A Christmas Crime

THE REBECCA ORANGE CASTLE COZY MYSTERY SERIES
BOOK EIGHT

VALERIE BRANDY

EMERALD LION PRESS

Published by: Emerald Lion Press. 23901 Calabasas Rd., Ste 2088, Calabasas, CA 91302. emeraldlionpress@gmail.com

ISBN: 978-1-964161-89-1

Editing provided by Sharon Lennon-Mehlschau.

Printed in the United States of America. To request permission to use passages from this book in any context other than a review, please contact the publisher at emeraldlionpress@gmail.com.

Visit the author's website at: www.valeriebrandy.com

✳ Formatted with Vellum

CHAPTER
One

TRAINS ARE PEACEFUL, I think to myself. *I could get used to this.* Beneath my feet, the click-clack of wheels over metal vibrates through my legs. Over the past twenty-four hours, the sound has become a soothing one. I didn't expect to like traveling by train so much, but there's something nostalgic and quaint about it.

The honeymoon suite of the *Monrovian Royal Express* lurches gently as our train climbs higher into the mountains, snow-covered pines rushing past panoramic windows. Beside me, Joe— my 250-pound Tibetan Mastiff dog— leans into my leg, letting out an enormous burp. Next to him, an empty silver bowl that contained caviar just moments ago rattles in pace.

"Joe, there's no burping in the honeymoon suite," I say, taking a sip of champagne from the flute in my hand. Next to Joe, Luma— the Duke's collie who's just finished her own bowl of caviar— picks up a paw and boops Joe on the nose, as if she's enforcing Royal behavior. She gives him a look that says, *Can you try to act dignified for once?*

Joe burps again in response.

Beside me, the Duke— Jack— my *husband*, which still feels strange to say— raises his glass to mine. He clinks the glasses together, wearing that quiet smile that made me fall for him in the first place.

"Actually," Jack corrects me, "I think the Duke and Duchess of Atwood passed a law saying dog burps are *encouraged* on trains. Didn't you hear? They just got married this year, if you believe the tabloids." He winks at me, telling our own story as if it belongs to strangers.

The Duke and Duchess, I think. Royal titles are another concept I'm still getting used to, along with having security follow you everywhere and using multiple forks at dinner.

"I heard the Duke is quite handsome," I say, taking another sip of my champagne. "But I don't follow tabloids much."

"Your first lie to me. A good sign for our marriage, I think," Jack says, his eyes crinkling at the corners. He knows I love a good tabloid, preferably read in a bubble bath and full of questionable gossip.

Joe lets out a grumble of contentment as he licks the last bits of caviar from his tiny silver dish. Then, he moves his massive golden bulk to sprawl across a velvet ottoman that's probably an antique from some royal collection. Next to him, Luma curls up daintily on her own cushion. Her eyes dart between all of us as if she's waiting for a Royal attendant to brush her fur.

"She's going to get spoiled," I say, nodding toward Luma. "She fits the Royal lifestyle more than any of us do."

Jack laughs. "Says the woman who has Chef Renauld prepare her dog a Prince's meal every night."

I reach over to scratch Joe behind his ears, and he lets out a contented sigh. "Joe's earned it. Getting in trouble all the time is hard work."

The train's honeymoon suite is over-decorated in the best

possible way. Wood-paneled walls inlaid with gold. Plush burgundy seating. A dining nook, a separate bedroom visible through French doors, and even a small bathroom with— I kid you not— a clawfoot tub. The windows stretch from floor to ceiling, offering unobstructed views of the mountain land-scape. It's like someone took a five-star hotel room and shrunk it down to fit on a train.

"This is nice," I say, leaning into Jack's shoulder. "Just us. No staff, no royal duties. We finally get some time alone—"

Just then, the door to our compartment slides open, and a familiar voice fills the cabin.

"Can you believe how big the waffles are?" Maggie exclaims, standing in the doorway with wide eyes. "We just got room service and they're as big as my head!"

Jack laughs, his arm tightening around my shoulders. "Well... *almost* alone."

I shoot him a look that's half amusement, half exaspera-tion. When we planned this honeymoon, I had visions of just the two of us cuddled up in front of a fireplace, sipping hot chocolate, and generally doing the things newlyweds do. I should have known better. Being a Royal means you can never be truly alone.

Maggie steps fully into our compartment, her blonde braids bouncing with each movement. She's traded her usual professional attire for a casual sweater and jeans, but still manages to look like she could organize a gala at a moment's notice. Her tablet is tucked under her arm— the electronic appendage she's never without.

"Sorry to interrupt," she says, not looking sorry at all. "But I wanted to check if you'd like breakfast delivered here or if you're planning to join us in the dining car?" Her eyes drift to the champagne and caviar. "Although I see you've already started."

"It's our honeymoon, Maggie," I say pointedly.

"I know, I know! And I promise Benjamin and I will stay *completely* out of your way." She mimes zipping her lips, then immediately unzips them to continue. "Besides, the Queen said it was either me or members of the Royal Guard, so I'm the better choice, right?"

Jack sighs with good humor. "She's not wrong."

I can't argue with that. When Jack told his aunt (the Queen) that we were planning a honeymoon without security, she practically had a coronary. As third in line for the Monrovian throne, Jack rarely goes anywhere without protection. After some loud whispering, they ultimately agreed on a compromise: Maggie would escort us on the trip as Royal liaison, reporting back and managing any security issues. The compromise felt like a win. I trust Maggie to be less obtrusive than Royal Guards, and it doesn't hurt having my best friend on the trip.

"Although," Maggie adds, shifting her weight from one foot to the other in that way she does when she's about to drop news she knows I won't like, "the Queen *did* insist I bring a little muscle along. She said she didn't feel confident I'd be able to handle terrorist threats and potential kidnappers on my own..."

"But you're so tough!" I add solemnly.

"Apparently not tough enough. So I had to ask for some help..."

She gestures toward the hallway behind her. A familiar voice floats in before we see its owner.

"These croissants are extraordinary. The butter actually tastes like butter, not that garbage they serve at the station."

Officer Basilier steps into view, and I nearly choke on my champagne. She's wearing flannel pajamas printed with tiny handcuffs and police badges, her hair sticking up at odd angles. She's holding a croissant in one hand and a steaming mug in the other.

"Officer Basilier?" I splutter. "What are you doing here?"

When we boarded the train last night, I thought Maggie and her new boyfriend— Benjamin, who owns the pet store in the village— were our only company.

Joe perks up at the sight of Officer Basilier, his tail thumping against the ottoman. For reasons I've never fully understood, my dog adores the petite police officer.

"Royal security," she says, taking a bite of her croissant and speaking through it. "Queen's orders. The Duke needs protection, even on his honeymoon." She gestures vaguely with her croissant. "Third in line for the throne and all that. And then *you* have to go and marry him and make everything even more public and weird. Might as well have painted a target on both your backs, Orange."

Jack leans forward, setting his champagne flute on the table, his expression surly. "I wasn't informed of this! Maggie, I must insist—"

"It's too late, the next station is our stop!" Maggie says, throwing her hands in the air before muttering, "This is why I waited to tell you until the train was too far gone…"

"Don't worry," Officer Basilier replies, brushing croissant crumbs from her pajama top. "I'll stay out of your way. It's *her* you need to worry about." She jerks her thumb toward Maggie, who looks affronted.

"Me? I'm the definition of discretion!"

Jack and I exchange a look that sends us both into laughter. Maggie's many talents don't include being discreet.

"I'll be in the breakfast car if anyone needs me," Officer Basilier announces, turning to leave. "Though I sincerely hope no one does. I need a vacation every now and then too, you know…"

As she disappears down the corridor, I turn to Maggie with raised eyebrows. "Anyone else hiding in the train that I should know about? The royal gardener? The Queen's third cousin twice removed?"

"Just Benjamin," she says brightly, smiling at the mention

of her new love interest. "He's finishing his waffle and boring me with facts about what movies were shot in the small town we're heading to."

Luma trots over to the door, peering out as if hoping to catch a glimpse of more visitors, then returns to curl up next to Joe on the ottoman. The dogs, at least, seem unfazed by our growing entourage.

Maggie makes herself comfortable on one of the plush armchairs, pulling out her tablet. "Speaking of the town, I've been doing more research on where we're going, and it's absolutely magical."

I can't help but feel a flicker of excitement at Maggie's research. I'd picked the Château des Flocons after stumbling across it online— a fairytale castle perched on a snowy mountain, converted into a boutique ski resort. I knew immediately it was the perfect spot for a honeymoon, and tasked Maggie with doing a deeper dive and booking the reservations.

"It's an old castle that's been in the same family for generations," Maggie continues, swiping through images on her tablet. "The current owner, Mr. Jacoby, inherited the title of Lord but prefers to be called Mister. He's like you, Jack," Maggie nods. "He likes to think of himself as a regular person."

"That's me," Jack laughs, throwing his hands in the air. "Just constantly thinking of myself as an ordinary person!"

"The castle has seven bedrooms total," Maggie continues. "One for Mr. Jacoby, one for his manager Freya, one for *her* son, and four for guests. You'll have the best suite, of course," Maggie adds, as if there was any question.

"It looks smaller than Castle Atwood," Jack observes, glancing at the photos over Maggie's shoulder.

"Much smaller," she agrees. "More intimate. And completely charming. The manager— Freya— has done all the interior decorating— lots of bookshelves, plush furniture, warm lighting. It's cozy rather than grand."

That sounds perfect to me. After months of living in the sprawling Castle Atwood with its countless rooms and corridors, something more human-sized appeals to my American sensibilities.

"And it's walking distance to Floconville Village," Maggie continues. "The most adorable little mountain town you've ever seen. Cobblestone streets, cafes, pubs, the works. Everything's decorated for Christmas right now."

Jack slides closer to me on the sofa. "It sounds perfect." His hand finds mine, our fingers intertwining naturally.

"Oh!" Maggie's eyes widen with excitement. "And the best part— Mr. Jacoby has given us tickets to the Glacial Games!"

"The what now?" I ask.

"The Glacial Games! Only the biggest winter sports competition in Monrovia!" Maggie looks at me like I've just admitted to never having heard of Christmas. "It's happening right on the slopes behind the château. Skiers from all over Europe compete. Benjamin is beside himself with excitement."

Of course he is. Benjamin is obsessed with all things athletic and adventurous— a byproduct of his fixation on American movies.

"Convenient, isn't it?" I ask, arching an eyebrow. "*You* wanted to see the Glacial Games and just so happened to find a way to go on our honeymoon with us?"

Maggie has the grace to look slightly embarrassed. "The Queen really *did* insist I come along," she protests. "The tickets are just a... happy coincidence!"

"Mhm," I hum, unconvinced.

"Don't worry," she hastens to add. "Benjamin and I will be at the games most of the time. You won't even know we're there."

"Except at breakfast," Jack points out. "And apparently, when room service delivers oversized waffles."

"Well, yes, except then." Maggie stands, clutching her tablet to her chest. "I knew you wouldn't want tickets,

Rebecca, because you hate sports, but if you two decide you do want to come, I can ask Mr. Jacoby to request—"

"No thanks," I tell her, shaking my head. "We just want a honeymoon with privacy. And no murder."

"Cheers to that!" Jack says.

Maggie nods, packing up her tablet. "Anyway, I should get back to Benjamin before he orders more food. The train staff are starting to give him looks."

As she heads toward the door, she pauses. "Oh, did I mention the château has issues with the plumbing? Mr. Jacoby said something always seems to be breaking due to the building's age. But the location makes up for it! It will still be a super romantic honeymoon even if there's sewage involved. Don't worry."

With that parting informational bomb, she's gone, sliding the compartment door closed behind her.

I turn to Jack, who's watching me with amusement dancing in his eyes. "So much for our private getaway," I say.

He pulls me closer, pressing a kiss to my temple. "We'll find our moments. Look at it this way," he gestures toward the window, where the snow-covered landscape continues to pass by. "We're headed to a beautiful château in the mountains. There will be skiing, hot chocolate by the fire, Christmas decorations everywhere..."

"Faulty plumbing and possible sewage," I add.

"That too." He laughs. "But we'll be together. That's what matters."

Joe lifts his massive head from the ottoman, letting out a soft woof of agreement. Luma, not to be outdone, gives a delicate bark of her own.

"See? Even the dogs agree." Jack refills our champagne flutes. "To our unconventional honeymoon. May it be memorable for all the right reasons."

I clink my glass against his, letting myself relax into the moment. "To our unconventional honeymoon."

As we sip our champagne, I gaze out at the winter wonderland passing by outside. The train climbs higher, carrying us toward the Château des Flocons, our eccentric entourage, and whatever adventures await us in the snowy mountains of Monrovia.

CHAPTER
Two

THE TRAIN WHISTLE cuts through the crisp mountain air as we pull into Floconville station. Through frosted windows, I catch my first glimpse of the village— a cluster of charming buildings with snow-covered rooftops nestled in a valley between towering, pine-dotted mountains. It looks like someone took a snow globe, shook it vigorously, and then placed us inside the perfect winter wonderland. Jack squeezes my hand as we gather our things.

"It's even prettier than the pictures," I murmur, pressing my nose against the cold glass like a child.

Jack leans in beside me, his breath fogging the window. "And look— no paparazzi. Just snow and beauty."

"And us," comes Maggie's voice from directly behind us, causing both Jack and me to jump slightly. "Don't forget us!"

I turn to find Maggie standing in the doorway, already dressed in a puffy pink coat with a matching hat and mittens. She looks like she's starring in a winter fashion catalog. Benjamin stands beside her, struggling to zip up his own coat while balancing Joe's leash in one hand and a croissant in the other.

"We couldn't possibly!" I say, laughing.

The train jerks to a complete stop, and Joe, who had been lounging across a seat near the doorway, stands up and stretches his enormous frame, knocking Benjamin's croissant to the floor. Benjamin looks at it mournfully.

"*Merde!* I wasn't finished with that," he says, his accent more pronounced when he's disappointed.

"Joe was helping you watch your figure," Officer Basilier comments, appearing in the hallway behind Benjamin. She's dressed in what appears to be tactical winter gear, complete with heavy boots that look capable of kicking down doors. "Let's get moving. I don't like being stationary in an unsecured location."

Jack rolls his eyes at me behind Officer Basilier's back. "It's a village of maybe 800 people, Basilier," he says, his tone sharp. "Not exactly a security hotspot." Jack still hasn't forgiven Officer Basilier for locking me in jail not too long ago. But that was when we were just getting to know each other. Now, we're practically old friends.

"That's exactly what they *want* you to think, Your Grace," she replies, her eyes scanning the platform outside our window like she's expecting snipers.

We gather our belongings, which in my case means simply grabbing my duffel bag and Joe's leash. Jack has a similar bag, though I know from experience his contains far more expensive items than mine. Luma sits patiently at Jack's feet, her tail swishing back and forth across the polished train floor.

"Oh, Rebecca," Benjamin says, stepping forward as I reach for Joe's leash. "Please, allow me to handle the dogs. You're on your honeymoon! You should be relaxing, not worrying about animal care."

I hesitate, glancing at Joe, who's eyeing Benjamin with what I can only describe as canine skepticism.

"That's really nice of you, Benjamin, but Joe can be a handful. His breed is one of the most stubborn in the world—"

"Nonsense! I own a pet shop. Animals are my specialty."

He puffs his chest out proudly. "And I've been watching Indiana Jones movies all week to prepare for adventure!"

I'm not entirely sure how Harrison Ford prepared Benjamin for dog-walking, but before I can protest further, he's taken both leashes from Jack and me. Joe gives me a look that clearly says, "Really? This guy?"

"Well... okay," I concede. "But remember, Joe doesn't always listen to commands from people he doesn't know well, and he weighs more than you do."

"And Luma gets distracted by small animals," Jack adds helpfully. "Especially squirrels."

Benjamin waves away our concerns. "They will be perfect angels for Uncle Benjamin, won't you?" He makes kissy noises at both dogs. Luma tilts her head like she's plotting a coup. Joe yawns, accidentally showcasing his enormous teeth.

"Let's move," Officer Basilier orders, already stepping onto the platform. She walks with her hand resting on her hip, uncomfortably close to her holstered gun.

After a brief walk down the hall, we make our way to the train's exit in a neat line behind Officer Basilier. She pokes her head out of the door and gives a hand signal that I assume means, " all clear." We file out after her, stepping from the warm train into the bracing mountain air. My breath clouds in front of me as I take in our surroundings. The platform is small and quaint, with wooden beams and a peaked roof, all dusted with fresh snow. Beyond it, the village of Floconville spreads out like a picture on a Christmas card.

A light show falls. Lampposts wrapped in evergreen garlands and twinkling lights line the cobblestone streets. Shop windows glow with warm light, and I spot a group of carolers in Victorian-style clothing gathering near the station exit, songbooks in hand.

"It's like we stepped into a Hallmark movie," I whisper to Jack.

"A what?" he asks, and I'm reminded once again of the cultural divide between us.

"Never mind. It's perfect."

As we make our way toward the exit, Benjamin strides ahead confidently with the dogs. For approximately three seconds, everything is fine. Then Luma spots something she deems a threat— possibly a squirrel, or just an interesting shadow— and lunges forward with all her dainty might.

Benjamin, unprepared for the sudden movement, is yanked forward so violently he nearly face-plants into the snow. He manages to keep his footing but is now being dragged at an alarming pace behind Luma's princess-like form. Joe, not wanting to be forgotten, begins pulling in the opposite direction toward a small child holding what appears to be a pastry.

"Oh no," I mutter, preparing to run after them.

Jack puts a restraining hand on my arm. "You *are* on your honeymoon. The dogs won't treat him too badly, right?"

"I could always use the whistle to call them both back to us," I agree. I've been training the dogs to recall with perfect precision over the past few months, and the dog whistle's sound can carry for miles. "They'd probably return without Benjamin, but that's fine."

I watch as Benjamin, now stretched between two determined dogs pulling in opposite directions, calls out desperately in French. I catch something about "Indiana Jones would not have this problem!" before he disappears around the corner of the station.

"Should we help him?" Maggie asks, looking torn between concern and amusement.

"Nope," Jack and I say in unison before sharing a smile.

We continue into the village, rolling our luggage trailing behind us on wheeled carts provided by the train attendants. Officer Basilier walks ahead, her head swiveling left and right like a security camera. Every few steps she pauses, scans the area, and then proceeds. It's like watching a one-woman military operation.

"Officer Basilier," Jack calls out, his voice carrying the subtle command of someone used to being obeyed. "You're drawing more attention to us than if you simply walked normally."

She glances back at us, frowning. "I'm doing my job, Your Grace."

"Your job is to blend in," he counters. "Not to make everyone think we're transporting the crown jewels through town."

Officer Basilier's frown deepens, but she does slow her pace, allowing us to catch up. "Fine. But I'm keeping my hand on my weapon."

"Why don't you just pull it out and wave it around?" I suggest. "That would really send a message."

She gives me a look that would wither most people, but after months of working together on cases, I've developed a certain immunity to her glares.

We continue down the main street of Floconville, and I'm struck by how thoroughly the village has embraced the Christmas season. Every storefront is decorated with wreaths, lights, or festive displays. A massive Christmas tree stands in the center of what appears to be the town square, its branches heavy with ornaments and snow. Children throw snowballs near a fountain that's been turned off for the season, now serving as an impromptu snow fort.

We pass a bakery with windows steamed up from the heat inside, showcasing rows of pastries and bread. Next door, a boutique displays handmade sweaters and scarves. Across the street, a bookshop with a sign in both French and English advertises "Hot Cocoa with Every Purchase."

"Oh, we have to go there," I say, pointing at the bookshop.

"Agreed," Jack says, following my gaze. "But first—" He nods toward a building with a wooden sign hanging above the door. The sign depicts a mug of something frothy next to what appears to be a ski pole. "That pub looks promising."

The pub's windows glow with golden light, and even from outside, I can hear laughter and the clink of glasses. A chalkboard sign out front advertises "Floconville's Best Mulled Wine" and "Hearty Mountain Fare."

"Perfect for après-ski," Jack says, looking like he's mentally already inside with a drink in hand.

"Or après-train," I suggest. "We haven't even made it to the château yet."

"Details," he waves dismissively, then catches my eye with a smile that still makes my heart skip. "We'll come back."

As we continue our exploration, I notice people glancing at our group— mainly at Officer Basilier, who still looks like she's guarding the president— but no one seems to recognize Jack. His usual regal bearing is well disguised under layers of winter clothing: a thick wool sweater, a heavy coat, and a knitted hat pulled down almost to his eyebrows. A scarf wrapped around the lower half of his face completes the incognito look.

"No one knows who we are," I observe quietly.

Jack's eyes crinkle above his scarf in what I know is a smile. "One of the benefits of winter clothing. For once, I'm just a tourist."

He turns to Officer Basilier. "See? No one recognizes us. You can relax."

"That's exactly when security threats are most likely to occur, Your Grace," she replies, scanning a group of elderly women who are admiring a window display of Christmas ornaments. "When you least expect it."

Jack sighs, his breath visible in the cold air. "If I get assassinated by grandmothers in Floconville, I promise you can say 'I told you so' at my funeral."

We round a corner, and Benjamin appears before us, looking harried. His hair is sticking up in all directions, his coat is halfway unzipped, and there's a smear of something that might be mud or chocolate on his cheek. He's still clutching both leashes, but now the dogs are walking calmly beside him, looking for all the world like they've never misbehaved in their lives.

"Everything okay?" I ask, trying not to laugh.

"Yes, yes, of course," Benjamin says, breathing heavily. "Just a small... cultural misunderstanding between me and the dogs. But we have reached an agreement now, haven't we?" He looks down at Joe and Luma, who both wag their tails innocently.

I know that look on Joe's face. It's the one he gets after he's won an argument.

"What did he make you give him?" I ask Benjamin.

Benjamin's eyes widen. "How did you know?"

"Twenty years of animal training. What was it?"

"A sausage," he admits. "From a man selling them on the corner. And part of a pretzel. And three cupcakes he stole from a display case. And I may have promised him a steak dinner later."

I pat Benjamin's shoulder. "Welcome to Joe's world. We all live in it; he just lets us visit sometimes."

As we continue down the main street, I notice colorful banners hanging from every lamppost. They all advertise something called "The Glacial Games," featuring images of skiers, snowboarders, and other winter athletes in action poses. One particularly large banner showcases a stern-faced man with dark hair falling artfully over one eye, holding a pair of skis. The text beneath identifies him as "Harris Hastings, Three-Time Euro Champion."

Maggie gasps when she sees it. "Oh my God, that's Harris Hastings!" Her voice rises to a pitch that makes both dogs look up in alarm. "He's so—" She's about to say 'cute,' but she catches Benjamin's eye and abruptly changes course. "— talented! So very *talented* at skiing."

Benjamin frowns slightly, looking between Maggie and the banner.

"He has good technique," Benjamin concedes, though his tone suggests he's not entirely impressed. "But I hear his turns are sloppy."

Maggie tears her eyes away from the banner. "Sloppy?! The man is a physical genius with the prowess of a jaguar."

I elbow her sharply in the ribs when Benjamin looks away, and she has the grace to look embarrassed.

"Ouch," she mouths at me, rubbing her side.

"Sorry," I whisper back. "But your crush was showing."

"I don't have a crush," she whispers fiercely. "I was just appreciating athletic skill."

"Mhm. Like I appreciate Jack's diplomatic abilities."

Maggie snorts, then quickly composes herself when Benjamin glances our way.

We pass by a coffee shop that catches my eye. Unlike the others, this one has an actual pine tree growing up through the center of the café, decorated from top to bottom with twinkling lights and ornaments. Tables surround the tree in a circle, and customers sit sipping from steaming mugs, looking perfectly content.

"*Café Chaleur, Cœurs Chaleureux,*" Maggie reads the store name aloud. "It means *Warm Coffee, Warm Hearts.*

"We need to go there," I say, pointing at the coffee shop.

She nods enthusiastically. "Coffee around a Christmas tree? Yes, please."

In the distance, beyond the edges of the village, I can make out the ski slopes. They rise up from behind the buildings, white tracks cutting through dark green forests. At the very top, I spot what must be the Château des Flocons— a fairytale castle with pointed turrets and glowing windows, perched dramatically on the mountainside.

"There it is," Jack says, following my gaze. "Our home for the next week."

"It looks like something from a storybook," I say.

We reach the edge of the village, where the cobblestone street meets a snow-covered driveway that winds up toward the mountain. A sleek black town car is parked there, its engine running. A driver in a neat uniform stands beside it, holding a sign that reads "Duke and Duchess of Atwood."

"So much for anonymity," Jack mutters.

Officer Basilier marches up to the man with the sign and whispers something in his ear. He immediately crumples the sign into a ball and shoves the paper in his pocket. Officer Basilier shoots Maggie a dirty look.

"I arranged for the sign to be small," Maggie says defensively.

The driver spots us and straightens.

"Your Grace, Your Grace," he says, bowing slightly to both of us. I'm still not used to being addressed that way. "Welcome to Floconville. I'm Claude, and I'll be driving you to the château."

"Thank you, Claude," Jack says warmly. "Is there room for all of us and the dogs?"

Claude looks at our group, his eyes widening slightly at the size of Joe, but he recovers quickly. "Of course, Your Grace. We've brought the extended vehicle, as requested by Ms. Lefevere."

"Maggie thinks of everything," I say, giving her an appreciative nod.

"I try," she replies with a modest shrug that doesn't quite hide her satisfaction.

As we approach the car, I take one last look back at Floconville. The snow continues to fall gently, adding to the magical quality of the village. Lights twinkle from every window, smoke curls from chimneys, and the sounds of distant laughter and music float through the air.

For a moment, I forget about our entourage, about being a

Duchess, about everything except how perfect this moment feels. Jack's hand finds mine, and he squeezes it gently.

"Ready for the next part of the adventure?" he asks.

I smile up at him. "With you? Always."

We pile into the car— dogs, security officer, best friend, and boyfriend included— and begin the winding journey up to the château, where our unconventional honeymoon awaits.

CHAPTER
Three

THE TOWN CAR winds its way up the mountain, each turn revealing more breathtaking scenery. Snow-laden pine trees line the narrow road, their branches bowing under the weight of fresh powder. Château des Flocons slowly comes into view. Even from a distance, it's exactly as magical as the photos Maggie found online, its glowing windows promising warmth against the winter chill.

"It's beautiful," I whisper, feeling Jack's hand cover mine on the seat between us.

"Worth the trek?" he asks, his voice low enough that only I can hear.

"Definitely," I reply with a wry smile. In the front seat, Officer Basilier sits ramrod straight, her eyes scanning the landscape for potential threats to our safety.

The car slows as we approach the château's entrance— a grand archway festooned with evergreen garlands and twinkling lights. Two enormous Christmas trees flank the massive wooden doors, each decorated with red and gold ornaments that catch the late afternoon light. A fresh dusting of snow covers everything like confectioner's sugar on a holiday dessert.

Claude pulls the car to a stop on the circular driveway. "We have arrived, Your Graces," he announces, his formal tone a reminder that we haven't quite escaped the trappings of royal life.

As we exit the vehicle, Joe practically drags Benjamin out behind him, eager to investigate this new territory. Luma follows more regally, her tail held high as she prances through the snow. The cold air bites at my cheeks, but it's refreshing after hours of travel.

"I thought you said it was small," I say to Maggie, gazing up at the château. While not as sprawling as Castle Atwood, it's hardly the cozy château I'd been imagining.

"Small for a castle," Maggie clarifies. "Enormous for, you know, normal people housing."

The front doors swing open before we reach them, revealing a woman in her mid-thirties with her brown hair pulled back in a practical ponytail. She wears a simple black skirt and burgundy sweater— professional but approachable — and a warm smile that immediately puts me at ease.

"Welcome to Château des Flocons!" she calls out, her voice carrying across the snowy courtyard. "I'm Freya Varga, property manager. You must be the Duke and Duchess of Atwood." She curtsies slightly as we approach, but there's none of the obsequiousness I've grown to expect from people meeting Jack for the first time.

"Please, call me Rebecca," I say, extending my hand. "And this is Jack. We're trying to keep the titles to a minimum on our honeymoon."

Freya's smile widens as she shakes my hand. "Of course. Mr. Jacoby will appreciate that. He's not one for formalities either."

We follow her inside, and I'm immediately enveloped by warmth and the scent of cinnamon, pine, and something delicious baking. The entrance hall is smaller than Castle Atwood's, but what it lacks in size, it makes up for in charm.

A stone fireplace dominates one wall, a cheerful fire crackling behind an ornate screen. The floors are polished wood, covered by richly colored rugs. Above us, wooden beams cross the ceiling, from which hang evergreen garlands and vintage glass ornaments.

"This is gorgeous," I breathe, turning in a slow circle to take it all in.

Freya leads us to a reception area off to the side— a beautiful antique desk surrounded by comfortable-looking chairs. As she moves behind the desk, a boy of about twelve darts out from a doorway behind her.

"Mom, what's for dinner? I'm starving, and I need to talk to you about my school—"

"Not *now*—" Freya says, shooting a meaningful glance at our group. "I told you, later—"

"But my school! You promised we'd talk about it—" He stops short when he notices us, his eyes widening as they land on Joe. "Whoa. That's the biggest dog I've ever seen! He's as big as a lion."

"Noah," Freya says, a note of gentle reproach in her voice. "This is the Duke and Duchess of Atwood and their guests. They'll be staying with us for the week."

Noah tears his gaze away from Joe long enough to give us a quick once-over. "Cool," he says, then immediately returns his attention to my dog. "Can I pet him?"

"If it's okay with Ms. Rebecca," Freya says, giving me an apologetic smile.

Next to Joe, Luma makes a huffing sound then walks away to stand beside Jack, almost as if she's offended at not being selected for attention.

"Of course," I reply. "Joe loves attention. Just approach slowly— he's friendly, but he can be overwhelming."

While Noah cautiously approaches Joe (who licks him on the face), Freya turns to a cabinet behind the desk and withdraws several large, ornate golden keys. Each one looks like it belongs in a museum— heavy and intricate, with a different decorative handle.

"We keep things traditional here," she explains, laying the keys on the desk. "Mr. Jacoby believes some modern conveniences take away from the château's character." She smiles ruefully. "Though I've convinced him that indoor plumbing and electricity were acceptable compromises."

"Speaking of plumbing," Maggie interjects, "you mentioned some... issues?"

Freya sighs. "The pipes are original to the building in some sections. We do our best, but occasionally there are... incidents. Nothing to worry about for your stay, I'm sure."

Jack and I exchange a glance that says we're both remembering Maggie's ominous "sewage" comment from the train.

"These are your keys," Freya continues, handing them out one by one. "The Snowflake Suite for the Duke and Duchess, the Pine Room for Ms. Lefevere and Mr. Leblanc, and the Hearth Room for Officer Basilier."

I turn my key over in my hand, feeling its weight. The handle is shaped like a snowflake, tiny details carved into the metal.

"Let me show you around before you settle in," Freya offers, coming back around the desk. She ruffles Noah's hair as she passes him. "We'll talk about dinner after I've finished the tour, okay?"

Noah nods absently, now sitting cross-legged on the floor with Joe's massive head in his lap.

"The château has seven bedrooms total," Freya explains as we begin our tour. "Mr. Jacoby's quarters, my son's room, my room, and four guest rooms, all of which are occupied this week."

We move through a formal dining room with a long table set for twelve, and a sitting room where another fireplace crackles invitingly. Every room is decorated for Christmas, with garlands, poinsettias, and vintage ornaments tastefully arranged. It's elegant without being ostentatious.

"Besides your group," Freya continues as we climb a curved staircase to the second floor, "we have Harris Hastings and his girlfriend, Pink Patricia, staying in the Crystal Room." She nods toward a closed door at the end of the hallway. "They arrived yesterday for the Glacial Games."

Maggie makes a sound that's somewhere between a gasp and a squeal. "I knew it! I suspected they were dating when I saw them together at the European Summer Charity Ball, but it wasn't confirmed! Oh my God, if Zacharia at the newsstand knew about this..."

Benjamin looks at her with raised eyebrows.

"For... journalistic purposes," Maggie adds hastily. "Not that I care personally."

"Who's Pink Patricia?" I ask, genuinely confused.

Maggie turns to me, eyes wide with disbelief. "You don't know Pink Patricia? The YouTube sensation? She's famous for her travel vlogs and her signature pink outfits. She's always in pink—hence the nickname. No one knows if Pink is her first name or if Patricia is, and she never clarifies." Maggie lowers her voice to a whisper. "She has fourteen million subscribers."

"Oh," I say, as if this explains everything, though it means nothing to me. "And Harris is...?"

"The skier," Jack supplies. "The one on the banners in town. The three-time champion Maggie thinks is cu—" Jack clears his throat, "— I mean... *talented.*"

"Four-time champion, actually," comes a voice from behind us. We turn to find a young woman standing in the hallway, dressed in—what else?—a pink velour tracksuit embellished with rhinestones spelling out "Sleigh Queen" across the chest. Her blonde hair is pulled into a high ponytail, and she's holding her phone out in front of her as if recording.

"Hi, followers!" she chirps to her phone. "I've just run into the Duke and Duchess of Atwood at our alpine château! Royalty alert! Don't forget to like and subscribe!" She lowers the phone slightly, but I notice she's still recording. "I'm Pink Patricia. It's so amazing to meet you!"

Maggie looks like she might faint from excitement. Officer Basilier looks like she wants to arrest Pink Patricia on the spot. "There will be absolutely *no* recording the Royals this weekend!" Officer Basilier says, disgusted.

"Lovely to meet you," Jack says smoothly, falling back on years of royal training for uncomfortable public encounters. "We're just getting settled in."

"This is perfect content for my Personal Encounters series," Pink Patricia continues, circling us with her phone. "My subscribers are going to freak out when they see this!"

Jack's smile tightens slightly. "Actually, as our security officer said, we'd prefer to keep a low profile during our stay. It's our honeymoon."

Pink Patricia's eyes widen. "A royal honeymoon? Even better! I could do a whole series on—"

"No," Jack and I say simultaneously.

Pink Patricia pouts for a moment, then shrugs. "Fine, fine. I can respect privacy." She doesn't lower her phone, though. "But if you change your mind, I'd love to collaborate! My château tour video has already hit two million views in just 24 hours!"

With that, she blows us a kiss and disappears back down the hallway, still filming herself.

"Sorry about that," Freya says once Patricia is out of earshot. "She's been recording everything since she arrived. Mr. Jacoby has had to remind her several times that other visitors might not want to be in her videos."

"It's fine," Jack assures her, though I can see the tension in his shoulders. He values his privacy, especially now.

"Let me show you to your rooms," Freya says, leading us

further down the hall. "The Snowflake Suite is our finest accommodation— perfect for a honeymoon."

As we continue the tour, I catch Jack's eye. He gives me a small smile that says, "Well, this should be interesting." As Freya opens the door to our suite and I glimpse the four-poster bed, the private fireplace, and the balcony overlooking the snow-covered mountains, I can't help but feel a flutter of excitement. *I'm on my honeymoon.* I never thought I'd get married, let alone to someone as amazing as Jack. There's a padding sound behind me, and Joe and Luma appear, side-by-side. Everyone I love is together, and the day has been so perfect so far— it feels like absolutely nothing can go wrong.

———

After a brief tour of the rest of the guest rooms, Freya returns our group to the lobby. We're now fully-versed in the castle layout, including the location of the kitchen and bathrooms. We're about to part ways, but Maggie steps forward with a hopeful look. She adjusts her tablet under her arm and smiles brightly at Freya. "This is all absolutely lovely," she says. "I was wondering, could we possibly meet with Mr. Jacoby? When I booked the honeymoon suite for the Duke and Duchess, he promised Benjamin and me tickets to the Glacial Games."

Freya nods, checking her watch. "Certainly! He should be in the library right now. He mentioned he was going to polish the nutcracker."

"The nutcracker?" I ask, picturing a small wooden toy soldier with a gaping mouth.

"Oh, it's not just any nutcracker," Freya explains, her eyes lighting up. "It was carved by hand over three hundred years ago! It's a special collectible being auctioned to benefit the Monrovian Children's Foundation. All the athletes competing in the Glacial Games have signed it, including Harris Hastings. Mr. Jacoby estimates it will sell for at least €50,000 at the charity auction next week."

Benjamin lets out a low whistle. "That is one expensive nutcracker."

"It's kept in a locked display case," Freya continues, leading us back down the hallway. "Mr. Jacoby has the key. He's been taking special care of it— polishing it daily, making sure the temperature and humidity in the library are perfect. He's quite proud to be hosting such a valuable item. Why don't you all come? I left the library out of our tour— you might as well see it."

"Jack's favorite room," I say, elbowing Jack in the ribs.

We follow Freya down the curved staircase, Joe and Luma padding quietly behind us. Officer Basilier has positioned herself directly behind Jack, presumably protecting us from unseen assassins.

"The library is one of the oldest rooms in the château," Freya tells us as we cross the entrance hall. "Some of the books date back to the 17th century. Mr. Jacoby's family has always been avid collectors."

She leads us to a set of heavy wooden doors, carved with intricate patterns of leaves and vines. Pushing them open, she steps aside to let us enter.

"Mr. Jacoby?" she calls. "You have visitors."

The library is everything I'd expect in a mountain château — floor-to-ceiling bookshelves, leather armchairs that have been broken in by generations of readers, a massive stone fireplace with a fire crackling merrily inside. A Christmas tree stands in one corner, decorated with antique ornaments and topped with a delicate glass star. The warm glow of lamps creates cozy pools of light throughout the room.

But something is wrong.

Joe and Luma both freeze at the threshold, hackles rising. Joe emits a low growl that I've rarely heard from him.

That's when I see it— or rather, *him*.

A figure lies sprawled on an ornate Persian rug in front of the fireplace. A plump man in a plaid vest, face-down and motionless. A small puddle of water surrounds him, reflecting the firelight in ominous ripples.

"Mr. Jacoby!" Freya's scream cuts through the stunned silence as she rushes forward.

Jack moves faster, getting to the prone figure before any of us. He kneels beside Mr. Jacoby, carefully turning him over. His face is slack, a trickle of blood running from a wound on his temple, darkening his gray mustache with crimson.

"He's breathing," Jack announces, his fingers pressed against Mr. Jacoby's neck. "Pulse is steady but weak."

I scan the room quickly, looking for details that could explain what happened. Water on the floor. Books still sitting safely in their shelves. Across the room, an empty display case stands open, its glass door swinging slightly.

"The nutcracker," I say, pointing. "It's gone."

Freya's hands fly to her face. "Oh my God. Who would do this? Who would hurt Mr. Jacoby?"

Officer Basilier pushes past me, her police training taking over. She quickly assesses the scene, then turns to Benjamin. "Call an ambulance, now."

Benjamin fumbles for his phone, hands shaking slightly. "Yes, of course, right away." He steps back into the hallway to make the call.

Officer Basilier pulls out her own phone. "I'll contact the Atwood Police Department and have them connect me with the Floconville authorities. We need to secure the scene."

Maggie moves to Freya's side, placing a comforting arm around the distraught manager's shoulders. "It's going to be okay," she says, though her eyes meet mine with a worried look. "He's breathing. We just need the ambulance to get here—"

I approach Jack, who's removed his scarf and folded it into

a makeshift pillow for Mr. Jacoby's head. "How bad is it?" I ask quietly. "Will he make it?"

"Head wound, but not too deep. Looks like he was struck from behind," Jack replies, his voice low. "Could have been much worse if the intent was to kill rather than incapacitate."

"So someone wanted him out of the way while they stole the nutcracker," I muse, crouching down to examine the water on the floor. "But why the water?"

Jack shakes his head. "I don't know. Maybe the killer panicked?"

"Someone tried to clean up something and did a poor job of it," I finish.

Joe and Luma have finally entered the room, though both dogs are staying close to the doorway, clearly uncomfortable with the scene before them. Joe keeps looking at me, then at Mr. Jacoby, as if asking what we should do.

I stand up and move to the display case, careful not to touch anything. The glass door hangs open, the lock clearly forced. Inside, on a velvet cushion, is nothing but a faint impression where the nutcracker once sat.

"Freya," I call over my shoulder, "who else knew about the nutcracker's value?"

She looks up, her face pale. "Everyone, I suppose. Mr. Jacoby wasn't secretive about it. All the guests know, the staff, even the people in the village. It was in the local paper last week."

Officer Basilier returns, slipping her phone into her pocket. "Ambulance is on its way. The local police will be here within twenty minutes." She surveys the room with a critical eye. "Nobody touches anything else until they arrive."

Freya wrings her hands, looking around at the chaos that has erupted in her carefully maintained château. "I can't believe this is happening," she says, her voice trembling. "Mr. Jacoby is the kindest man. He doesn't have enemies."

I exchange a look with Jack. Despite the excitement of our arrival and the beauty of the château, I'd been looking forward to a quiet week away from murder investigations and Royal Investigator duties. A chance to just be newlyweds in a winter wonderland. But looking at Mr. Jacoby's still form and the empty display case, I know that isn't in the cards for us.

Jack must read the conflict on my face because he gives me a small nod, his eyes crinkling at the corners in that way that makes my heart flip, even in the midst of a crisis. He turns to Freya, his voice calm and assured— the voice of the Duke of Atwood, not just my husband Jack.

"Don't worry, Freya," he says. "My wife, the Duchess, is on the case."

I shoot him a grateful look. This isn't exactly how I planned to spend our honeymoon, but at least my husband never tries to stop me from being myself.

Benjamin returns, slightly out of breath. "The ambulance is on its way. They said to keep him stable and not to move him.""Alright," I say, taking charge. "Officer Basilier, can you secure this room once the paramedics have taken Mr. Jacoby? We need to preserve any evidence." She nods, looking almost approving of my initiative. "Freya, we'll need a list of everyone who's been in the château in the last 24 hours. Maggie, could you help her with that?"

Maggie is already pulling out her tablet. "On it."

"Benjamin, could you take Joe and Luma back to our rooms? They're upset by the scene, and I don't want them contaminating any evidence."

Benjamin straightens, seemingly glad to have a task that takes him away from the unconscious man. "Of course, Rebecca. Come on, dogs."

As everyone moves to their assigned tasks, I turn back to the empty display case, my mind already racing through possibilities. Who took the nutcracker? Why attack Mr. Jacoby instead of just stealing it when the room was empty? And what's with the water on the floor?

Jack comes to stand beside me, his hand finding mine and giving it a reassuring squeeze. "So much for our crime-free honeymoon, I suppose?" he whispers.

"Well," I reply, squeezing back, "at least we're not bored."

Outside, the wail of an ambulance siren breaks the mountain silence. Snow continues to fall past the library windows, oblivious to the drama unfolding within the château's stone walls.

AN HOUR after finding Mr. Jacoby sprawled on the library floor, we're all gathered in the château's foyer like mismatched ornaments on a Christmas tree. Jack and I stand close together. Maggie clutches her tablet, using it as a shield. Benjamin nervously holds the dogs' leashes, keeping Joe and Luma surprisingly in line. Officer Basilier assumes a rigid stance, and Freya wrings her hands as she watches the front door. The ambulance has come and come, leaving Mr. Jacoby in the care of a medic who insisted he needed rest rather than a hospital stay. Now we're waiting for the local police, and judging by Freya's expression, their leader— Detective Freinz — isn't going to be bringing holiday cheer to our little crime scene.

"He's here," Freya says, her voice small as headlights sweep across the stained-glass panels flanking the entrance.

The château's massive front door swings open without a knock, admitting a gust of frigid air and a man who seems to absorb all warmth from the room. Detective Freinz strides in with the confidence of someone who already owns the place, flanked by two uniformed officers who remain silent in his shadow. His dark hair is slicked back, and his boots leave melting snow prints on the marble floor. His eyes perform a quick inventory of the space, lingering on the antique furniture as if assessing its value.

"Freya," he says, not bothering with pleasantries. His voice is wrapped in sandpaper. "Where is Lord Jacoby?"

Freya steps forward, visibly steeling herself. "Detective Freinz, thank you for coming so quickly. Mr. Jacoby is resting in the library. The medic is with him. He has a concussion but refused to go to the hospital."

"Typical," Detective Freinz mutters, then louder: "I need to speak with him immediately."

"Of course," Freya nods. "I can take you to him, but the medic said he needs rest and shouldn't be upset. And, with all due respect, your presence usually… *upsets* him."

The detective's laugh is brittle. "His precious château has been violated, and his overpriced nutcracker is missing. I'd say the upset ship has sailed."

Joe and Luma sense the tension, moving closer to Benjamin, who clutches their leashes tighter. Joe gives a soft whine, his eyes finding mine across the foyer. I give him a small nod to let him know everything's okay, even though I'm not convinced it is.

Detective Freinz turns his attention to Freya again, stepping closer in a way that makes her back up slightly. "This is exactly what I've been saying would happen for years. This place is a liability. A money pit with faulty plumbing, outdated wiring, and now apparently nonexistent security. How many times have I told Lord Jacoby he should sell while the property still has some value?"

Freya's chin lifts slightly. "The château has been in *Mr.* Jacoby's family for generations, Detective. He won't sell."

"Then he's a fool," Detective Freinz says flatly. "And this incident only proves my point. The château brings nothing but trouble to this community."

Maggie leans over and whispers in my ear, "Not exactly in the Christmas spirit, is he?"

Officer Basilier clears her throat pointedly, stepping forward with her shoulders squared. I recognize the posture — it's the same one she used when she first met me and thought I was interfering in her investigation at Castle Atwood.

"Detective Freinz," she says, extending her hand, which he ignores. "I'm Officer Basilier from the Atwood Police Department. Your chief should have received notification of my credentials by now."

The detective gives her a dismissive once-over. "Atwood? That's what— three hundred miles from here?"

"Two-hundred," Officer Basilier corrects. "I'm here providing security for the Duke and Duchess of Atwood." She gestures toward Jack and me. "But given the circumstances, I'd like to offer our assistance in your investigation."

Detective Freinz's eyebrows rise slightly at the mention of royalty, but his expression quickly reverts to indifference. "That won't be necessary, Officer. We can handle our own cases here in Floconville."

Officer Basilier persists, gesturing toward Maggie and me. "These are the Royal Investigators, Rebecca Orange and Maggie Lefevere. They've successfully solved multiple cases and—"

"I don't care if they've solved the mysteries of the universe," Detective Freinz cuts in. "This is my jurisdiction, and I don't need outside interference. Especially not from some bored Police Officer playing detective because she should have retired a few years ago."

I almost choke on my surprise at his rudeness. Beside me, Maggie's eyes widen, and her fingers fly over her tablet screen as if seeking digital refuge.

Officer Basilier looks stunned, her mouth opening and

closing wordlessly. I can't help myself— I give her a little elbow nudge.

"Not fun being on that side of the dismissal, is it?" I whisper. "Reminds me of someone I met when I first arrived at Castle Atwood."

She shoots me a glare, but there's a flash of recognition in her eyes. She knows exactly what I'm referring to. I assumed Officer Basilier would have brushed Freinz's comment off, but she seems rattled. The man managed to cut to the core, touching something deep within her. I almost want to give her a hug, but I know she'd hate the gesture, so I don't.

Officer Basilier stands frozen in place. As her software tries to reboot, the silence sits heavy in the air.

I've never seen anyone get to her, I think. *This man just broke Officer Basilier.*

Thankfully, Jack clears his throat to cut the tension.

"Detective Freinz," Jack says, stepping forward. The subtle shift in his posture is something I've come to recognize— he's transitioning from Jack, my husband, to the Duke of Atwood, royal authority figure. His voice takes on that pleasant-but-unmistakably-commanding tone that makes people instinctively stand straighter. "While I appreciate your dedication to your jurisdiction, I must insist that the Royal Investigators and Officer Basilier be allowed to conduct their own parallel investigation."

Detective Freinz's eyes narrow. "There is no possibility such a thing can be allowed, Your Grace—"

"It's not a request," Jack continues smoothly. "As a member of the Royal Family present at the scene of a crime, I have the right to ensure that any potential threats to royal safety are thoroughly investigated by personnel I trust. Monrovian law is quite clear on this matter."

Maggie's tablet practically materializes in front of her face. "Statute 457-B, paragraph 3," she reads aloud, "'In cases where a member of the Royal Family is present at the location of a crime, said royal may request that Royal Security conduct an independent investigation to ensure no threat exists to the Royal Family.' Enacted in 1887 after the Duchess of Westmoreland's earrings were stolen from her hotel room."

Detective Freinz's face darkens to an alarming shade of red. "Fine," he says through clenched teeth. "But stay out of my way. And I speak to Lord Jacoby first."

Jack inclines his head in gracious acknowledgment of a battle won. "Of course, Detective. We wouldn't dream of impeding your investigation."

The detective grunts and turns to Freya. "Take me to Lord Jacoby. Now."

As Freya leads Detective Freinz toward the library, Jack turns to Benjamin. "Benjamin, would you mind taking the dogs back to our suite? I think I'll join you and give Rebecca and the others space to work."

Benjamin straightens, visibly relieved to have a reason to exit. "Of course, Your Grace. Come on, Joe— Luma—"

Jack gives my hand a quick squeeze. "Try not to solve it before dinner," he whispers. "I was hoping for at least one romantic meal on our honeymoon."

I smile up at him. "No promises."

As Benjamin leads the dogs away and Jack follows, Joe suddenly pulls free from Benjamin's grasp and trots to my side, sitting down firmly as if to announce his intention to stay. His amber eyes lock with mine, and I swear I can read his thoughts: *You're not doing this without me.*

"He *is* part of the Royal Investigators," Maggie says.

Joe's tail thumps against the marble floor in agreement.

"Wouldn't have it any other way," I say, scratching behind his ears. "Ready to catch a nutcracker thief, big guy?"

Joe's answering woof echoes through the foyer as we follow Detective Freinz's wet footprints toward the library and whatever clues await us there.

———

The library looks different now than it did an hour ago. The medics have wiped away the water on the floor, and Mr. Jacoby is propped up in one of those well-worn leather armchairs instead of sprawled across the Persian rug. A fire still crackles in the massive stone fireplace, but the empty display case stands open like a wound, its glass door slightly ajar. Despite the head bandage and the blanket tucked around his legs, Mr. Jacoby looks surprisingly alert, his eyes brightening as we file into the room behind Detective Freinz.

"Lord Jacoby," Detective Freinz begins, pulling up a chair directly in front of the injured man without waiting for an invitation.

"Not you," Mr. Jacoby interrupts, his voice stronger than I expected. "Detective Freinz. You're not needed here. And as you know, I prefer *Mr.* Jacoby." His accent is refined, contradicting his words.

"And as *you* know," Detective Freinz counters, "I believe in being honest about who one is and the state of things. I see you've let the castle continue to fall into disrepair—"

"Not in front of my guests," Mr. Jacoby cuts Detective Freinz off. Mr. Jacoby's eyes find me, and recognition flickers across his face. "Ah! You must be the Duchess of Atwood. What a terrible way for me to meet you. I recognize you from the papers." His gaze shifts to Joe, who's staying close to my side. "And this magnificent fellow must be Joe. I've read about him, too."

I step forward, extending my hand. "Rebecca Orange. And yes, this is Joe. We were so sorry to find you in such a state earlier. How are you feeling?"

Mr. Jacoby takes my hand, his grip surprisingly firm for someone who's just been attacked. "Like I've been hit over the head, but I'll survive. The medic says I'm too stubborn to let one injury kill me." He looks past me to Maggie and Officer Basilier. "And these ladies are?"

"Maggie Lefevere, head of household at Castle Atwood and Royal Investigator," Maggie says, stepping forward with her tablet clutched to her chest. "We spoke on the phone when I booked the Duke and Duchess's honeymoon suite."

"Of course!" Mr. Jacoby's eyes light up. "I owe you those Glacial Games tickets, don't I? Though I fear with all this excitement, I've misplaced them somewhere."

"No rush," Maggie assures him, though I catch the flicker of disappointment in her eyes. "Your health is far more important."

"And I'm Officer Basilier, Atwood Police Department," Officer Basilier says.

"Good," Mr. Jacoby nods at her. "Maybe *you* can do some good here instead of leaving it all to Freinz."

Detective Freinz clears his throat loudly. "Now that we've all become acquainted, I need to ask you some questions about what happened here."

In the corner, Freya stands with her back against the wall, nervously watching the proceedings. Her fingers twist in the fabric of her sweater, and her eyes dart between Mr. Jacoby and Detective Freinz.

"Fine," Mr. Jacoby adjusts himself in the chair, wincing slightly. "Though I fear I won't be much use. My memory of the incident is rather fuzzy."

"Let's start with the nutcracker," Detective Freinz says, pulling out a small notebook. "What exactly made it so valuable?"

Mr. Jacoby's face brightens at the mention of the nutcracker. "It's a limited edition piece, hand-carved by Gustaf Hoffman, one of the most celebrated artists in Monrovian history. Only twelve were made, and fewer survived the passage of time. But what makes this one truly special is that it's been signed by every athlete competing in the Glacial Games this year. The idea was to auction it for the Monrovian Children's Foundation next week." He sighs. "We expected it to fetch at least 50,000 euros."

"That's quite a sum for a toy," Detective Freinz comments dryly.

"It's not a toy, *Detective*. It's a piece of Monrovian cultural history, enhanced by the signatures of our greatest winter athletes." Mr. Jacoby's voice takes on a passionate edge. "Harris Hastings alone— who's staying here, you know— his signature would add several thousand to the value."

"Tell me what you remember about the attack," Detective Freinz says, redirecting the conversation.

Mr. Jacoby's brow furrows. "I was in here around three o'clock, polishing the display case as I do every afternoon. I take great pride in keeping it pristine— fingerprints show up terribly on the glass." He gestures toward the ceiling. "I noticed water dripping from above— another issue with our ancient plumbing, I'm afraid. I looked up, and the next thing I knew, I was on my back with a splitting headache and..." He gestures toward the empty case. "Well, you can see the result."

"You didn't see or hear anyone enter the room?" Detective Freinz presses.

Mr. Jacoby shakes his head, then grimaces at the move-ment. "No. The château was quiet. Most of our guests were out watching the Glacial Games preliminary events."

"Could someone have been hiding in the room?" I ask. Joe has been slowly circling the library, nose to the ground, conducting his own investigation.

Mr. Jacoby considers this. "I suppose it's possible. The library is large, and there are alcoves between some of the bookshelves."

"Or perhaps someone used the plumbing leak as a distrac-tion," Maggie suggests, her investigator instincts clearly engaged.

"Or caused it deliberately," I add.

Detective Freinz shoots us an irritated look. "I'll ask the questions, if you don't mind."

A medic who's been quietly monitoring Mr. Jacoby from nearby steps forward. "I need to check your vitals again, sir, and change that bandage." He turns to Detective Freinz. "I must insist you keep this brief. Mr. Jacoby needs rest."

"Fine," Detective Freinz says tersely. "One more question. Who knew about the value of this nutcracker? Who would have a motive to steal it?"

Mr. Jacoby sighs. "Everyone, I'm afraid. I wasn't exactly secretive about it. It was just in the local newspaper." His eyes drift to the empty display case. "I never thought anyone would target the nutcracker in a way that led to violence, though. It's for charity, after all."

As the medic begins unwrapping the bandage around Mr. Jacoby's head, Joe approaches the chair. He moves slowly, deliberately, his massive frame surprisingly gentle as he extends his nose toward Mr. Jacoby's hand. Mr. Jacoby smiles and reaches out, letting Joe sniff his fingers before giving the dog a gentle pat on the head. Joe melts into his touch.

"Get the dog out of here," Detective Freinz says, trying to swat Joe away.

Joe crouches, baring his teeth at Detective Freinz and letting out a vicious growl that makes the man move back.

"What a magnificent animal," Mr. Jacoby says, grinning. He smiles as Joe trots back over to him and asks for pets as if nothing happened. "You know, I've always believed dogs are excellent judges of character."

Joe makes a contented sound, pressing his head more firmly against Mr. Jacoby's palm.

The medic finishes rewrapping Mr. Jacoby's head with fresh bandages. "You need to rest now, sir. No more questions for at least a few hours."

Detective Freinz stands, tucking his notebook away. "Fine.

I'll need to speak with everyone staying at the château. No one leaves the premises until I've conducted my interviews."

"Of course, Detective," Freya says from her position against the wall. "I'll arrange it."

As we prepare to leave the library, Detective Freinz turns to our group. "I'll handle this investigation *my* way. Stay out of it. And that goes for your *animals* as well. Royal statute or not, I won't have amateurs contaminating my crime scene."

Without waiting for a response, he stalks out, his boots leaving faint dirt marks on the expensive carpet.

Mr. Jacoby breathes a sigh of relief as soon as the Detective's figure disappears around the corner of the hallway. "He's gone. I apologize for that. Detective Freinz is a nightmare. Especially when it comes to this château. Please pay him no mind. I, for one, am exceedingly glad you're here. You have no idea."

As the medic helps Mr. Jacoby to his feet, we exit the library, leaving them to make their way slowly to his quarters. Once we're in the hallway with the door closed behind us, Freya's composure finally cracks.

"I can't believe this is happening," she whispers, her voice trembling. "First the attack on Mr. Jacoby, and now Detective Freinz..." She glances around nervously before continuing. "You should know— Detective Freinz has had it out for this place for years. He's filed countless complaints about building code violations, mostly related to our plumbing issues. He's been trying to get the château shut down."

"Why would he care so much about an old building's plumbing?" Officer Basilier asks, her police instincts clearly piqued.

Freya's voice drops even lower. "His brother is a real estate investor. He's been trying to buy the château from Mr. Jacoby for years. He wants to tear it down and build a modern resort hotel." Her eyes fill with tears. "I'm afraid he'll try to use this incident to finally force the sale. He'll say the place is dangerous and attracting crime. He's been appealing to the town's historical society to seize the Château via some old law—"

"Monrovian code number 6275," Maggie says, looking up from her tablet, where she's quickly searched the legal database for records. She reads aloud, "If a property of historic importance is not being well-maintained by the Lord or Lady who runs it, the townsfolk may reclaim the property and distribute it to a guardian of their choosing."

Freya nods. "Mr. Jacoby loves this place— it would break his heart."

Joe nudges against my leg, and I scratch behind his ears absently, my mind already racing with connections. A detective with a personal agenda. A valuable stolen item. An attack that conveniently occurred when most guests were away.

"Don't worry, Freya," I say. "We're going to find that nutcracker and figure out who attacked Mr. Jacoby— Detective Freinz's objections be damned."

Maggie's already typing notes into her tablet. "Royal Investigators officially on the case," she confirms, a determined smile spreading across her face.

"Count me in," Officer Basilier adds. "That detective needs an attitude adjustment."

Joe gives a soft woof of agreement, and just like that— the game is afoot.

CHAPTER
Five

I WAKE to the gentle crackling of a fire and the weight of Joe's massive paw draped across my ankle. Luma is curled beside him, her shallow breaths dainty compared to Joe's. For a moment, I forget where I am— the unfamiliar ceiling, the scent of pine and cinnamon in the air. Then I feel Jack's arm around my waist, his steady breathing warm against my neck, and it all comes rushing back. I'm in the Château des Flocons. On my honeymoon. As a duchess. With my husband, the Duke of Atwood. And there's a stolen nutcracker that needs finding.

Time to get to work.

I carefully extract myself from Jack's embrace and sit up, taking in the Snowflake Suite in the soft morning light. A four-poster bed dominates the room, draped in rich blue velvet that matches the snow-dusted mountains visible through the balcony doors. A fire flickers in the stone fireplace, casting dancing shadows across antique furniture that probably costs more than my entire apartment back home. Joe and Luma are curled together on plush dog beds near the hearth, a golden mountain and a sleek collie forming an unlikely pair.

Jack stirs beside me, his eyes opening slowly. He smiles that sleepy smile that still makes my heart do gymnastics, even after everything we've been through together.

"Morning, Duchess," he murmurs, reaching for my hand.

"Morning, Duke," I reply, leaning down to kiss him softly. "Sleep well?"

"Better than I have in months." He stretches, his dark hair tousled in a way that would never be permitted at official royal functions. This disheveled, private Jack is all mine, and I treasure these moments when the weight of the crown seems far away.

Just as Jack sits up, there's a gentle knock at the door. His eyes meet mine, and he grins mysteriously.

"Right on time," he says.

"You're expecting someone? I hope it's not Maggie with another waffle update."

Jack laughs, sliding out of bed and pulling on a plush robe embroidered with the château's logo. "Better than waffles, I promise."

He crosses to the door as I quickly pull on my own robe. When he opens it, a young staff member stands there with a large covered trolley that smells absolutely heavenly.

"Your breakfast, Your Grace," the young man says quietly. "As you requested."

Jack thanks him and slips him what I'm sure is an extravagant tip before wheeling the trolley in himself. The staff member disappears with a bow, and Jack turns to me with a triumphant smile.

"Breakfast in bed? No Maggie, no Officer Basilier, no missing Nutcrackers—just us."

Joe's massive head lifts at the smell of food, and Luma's tail begins to thump against her cushion. Jack laughs, wheeling the trolley closer to the bed.

"And the dogs, of course," he amends. "They're family, after all."

My heart swells at his words. For a man raised in rigid royal tradition, Jack's acceptance of Joe as part of our family has always meant the world to me.

I climb back into bed as Jack removes the silver dome covers to reveal a feast fit for, well, royalty. Fresh croissants, eggs Benedict, smoked salmon, a bowl of berries glistening with dew, a pot of coffee, and a bottle of champagne nestled in ice.

"Champagne for breakfast?" I ask, eyebrows raised.

"It's our honeymoon," Jack replies, popping the cork with practiced ease. "Royal tradition dictates champagne with every meal during the honeymoon week. Who am I to argue with tradition?"

"Since when do you care about tradition?" I tease, accepting a flute of bubbling champagne.

Jack sits beside me, lifting his glass. "Only the good ones. To my brilliant wife, who I suspect is already plotting how to solve the mystery of the missing nutcracker."

I clink my glass against his, feeling my cheeks warm. "Am I that predictable?"

"Completely." Jack grins, taking a sip. "And I wouldn't have it any other way."

We dig into the breakfast, and I have to admit it's spectacular. The eggs are perfectly poached, the hollandaise sauce velvety and rich, and the croissants so flaky they practically dissolve on my tongue. Jack slips pieces of salmon to Joe and Luma, earning appreciative whines from both dogs.

"You're spoiling them," I admonish with no real conviction.

"Royal dogs deserve royal treatment," he counters, tossing Joe another morsel.

We eat in comfortable silence for a few minutes, watching the snow fall gently outside our window. The mountains rise majestically beyond the glass, pristine white against a clear blue sky. It's picture-perfect, the kind of view that belongs on postcards and travel websites.

"So," Jack says finally, setting down his coffee cup. "About today."

I sigh. "I'm sorry. This isn't exactly how I planned to spend our honeymoon."

"Neither is watching sports with Benjamin, but here we are." Jack shrugs good-naturedly. "I've made plans with him to head down to the village later. There's a pub showing the Glacial Games, and he's desperate to see them."

I feel a rush of affection for this man who understands me so completely. "You don't have to do that," I say, though part of me is already mentally outlining interview questions for the château's residents.

"I know," Jack replies, taking my hand. "But I want to. You'll be miserable if you don't get to chase down this mystery, and frankly, I could use a few hours away from Pink Patricia's camera. Benjamin says she filmed him walking down the hallway last night."

"She didn't!"

"She did. Complete with commentary on his 'authentic Monrovian stride.'" Jack rolls his eyes. "Besides, you'll work faster without me hovering."

I squeeze his hand gratefully. "Have I told you lately that I love you?"

"Not since last night," he says with a sly grin that makes my stomach flip. "But I believe actions speak louder than words."

I lean across the breakfast tray to kiss him, careful not to knock over our champagne flutes. "Thank you for under-standing," I murmur against his lips.

"I married you knowing exactly who you are," Jack says, tucking a strand of hair behind my ear. "A woman who can't resist a good mystery. I'll take Luma with me to the village.

She loves a good walk in the snow. You, Maggie, and Officer Basilier can interrogate suspects to your hearts' content."

"It's not interrogation, it's interviewing," I correct him. "And thank you. I promise we'll have a proper romantic dinner tonight—just the two of us."

"I'll hold you to that," Jack says, leaning back against the pillows with his champagne. "Though I expect a full briefing on the case over dessert. I'm not entirely abandoning the investigation, you know."

I laugh, helping myself to another croissant. "Deal."

As we finish our breakfast with the snow falling peacefully outside, I find myself thinking how lucky I am. Not just because I married a duke and live in a castle—though that part still seems surreal— but because I found someone who accepts me completely. Someone who knows I can't turn off the investigator in me, even on our honeymoon, and loves me not despite it, but because of it.

And if solving the mystery of the missing nutcracker means I can get back to properly enjoying my honeymoon with my understanding husband, well, that's just killing two birds with one stone. Or maybe catching one thief with one duchess.

———

I descend the grand staircase with Joe padding beside me, his nails clicking against the polished wood. The château is quieter this morning— no ambulance sirens, no Detective Freinz barking orders, just the soft crackle of fires burning in various hearths and the distant clatter of breakfast dishes being cleared. It's almost peaceful enough to make me forget we're in the middle of an attempted-murder investigation. Almost, but not quite. Especially since Maggie and Officer Basilier are waiting at the bottom of the stairs looking like they're about to embark on a particularly intense episode of "Monrovian CSI."

"Good morning!" Maggie chirps, tablet already in hand and fingers flying across its surface. Her blonde braids are especially perky today, bouncing with each slight movement of her head. "I've already compiled a list of everyone present in the château at the time of the theft, cross-referenced with their known whereabouts, and created a timeline of events leading up to the discovery of Mr. Jacoby."

"I've gathered all potential witnesses and suspects in the dining room," Officer Basilier adds, her posture military-straight. She's wearing what appears to be tactical winter gear again, complete with pockets that could probably hold a small arsenal. "They're waiting for us now."

"Did you frisk them for weapons?" I ask, only half-joking.

Officer Basilier doesn't crack a smile. "No need. I've been observing them since 5 AM."

"Since 5 AM?" I repeat, eyebrows raising. "Do you ever sleep?"

"Sleep is a luxury," she replies seriously. "And unlike what Detective Freinz said, I'm not ready to retire. Or at least, not most days. Unless perhaps *you* think I should." There's a long, serious pause in which Office Basilier seems to be seriously considering the idea. "You *don't* think I should retire, do you?"

I exchange a glance with Maggie, who suppresses a smile. It seems like Detective Freinz really hit a nerve when he told Officer Basilier she should hang up her boots. "You can't retire because I don't know what I'd do without you," I say, patting Joe's head. "Jack's headed to the village with Benjamin and Luma later, so it'll just be us three—"

"Four," Maggie corrects, nodding toward Joe.

"—four," I amend, "handling the investigation today."

"Perfect," Officer Basilier says, turning on her heel. "Follow me."

We make our way through the entrance hall toward the dining room. Joe stays close to my side, his massive frame drawing stares from a passing staff member who flattens himself against the wall to give us room.

"Did Detective Freinz interview everyone last night?" I ask.

"Briefly," Maggie replies. "But he seemed more interested in finding building code violations than actual clues. He spent twenty minutes in the attic examining pipes."

"Not suspicious at all," I mutter.

Officer Basilier pushes open the ornate dining room doors with unnecessary force, causing everyone inside to jump. The long table that just last night held festive Christmas arrangements now looks like the world's most uncomfortable corporate meeting. Mr. Jacoby sits at the head, his bandaged head giving him a rakish appearance despite his plaid vest and kindly demeanor. To his right sits Freya, exhausted but composed, with her son Noah beside her, fidgeting with what appears to be a handheld video game. On Mr. Jacoby's left, Harris Hastings lounges with athletic grace, his dark hair artfully arranged to fall over one eye just like in his poster. Next to him, Pink Patricia perches on her chair, primed and perfect, as if she's appearing on a talk show interview.

"Good morning, everyone," I say as we enter. "Thank you for meeting with us."

"The Royal Investigators have arrived!" Pink Patricia announces to her phone. "Can the Duchess of Atwood solve the mystery of the missing Nutcracker? Tune in live to find out! And don't forget to like and subscribe!"

Harris Hastings rolls his eyes, slouching further in his chair. "Is this really necessary?" His voice is low and bored. "I have training in an hour."

"It *is* necessary," Officer Basilier says sharply. "A crime has been committed."

Joe trots around the table, sniffing each person carefully as

I take a seat across from Harris. Maggie slides into the chair beside me, immediately setting up her tablet like she's preparing to take minutes for a board meeting. Officer Basilier remains standing, positioned by the door as if she suspects someone might try to escape.

"First of all," I begin, "I want to thank you for your cooperation. We're trying to help Mr. Jacoby recover the nutcracker and find out who attacked him."

"I thought that detective with the attitude was handling the investigation," Harris comments, his fingers drumming impatiently on the table.

"Detective Freinz is conducting the official police investigation," I confirm. "We're running a parallel inquiry under Royal authority."

"Ooh, like good cop, bad cop!" Pink Patricia exclaims, adjusting her phone's angle. "Except it's grumpy detective, pretty duchess!"

I ignore the comment and continue, "I'd like to start by asking if anyone heard any unusual noises or saw people coming or going prior to the attack on Mr. Jacoby."

Noah's head pops up from his game. He twitches in his seat, his face flushing red. Then, he volunteers: "I saw a man in the kitchen. It was someone I'd never met before."

Freya looks surprised. "When was this, Noah?"

"Yesterday afternoon, before I went to study at Antoine's house. Around two, I think."

I glance at Maggie, who's already typing this information into her tablet. "Can you describe this person?" I ask.

Noah shrugs. "Regular looking. Uhm, he had a hat on. They were arguing about something."

"I'll speak with the kitchen staff," Maggie murmurs, making a note.

"Mr. Jacoby," I say, turning to our host, "who exactly knew about the nutcracker and its value?"Mr. Jacoby sighs, adjusting his bandage slightly. "As I told Detective Freinz, practically everyone. It was featured in the local paper, mentioned on Radio Floconville, and I'm afraid I've been rather enthusiastically showing it off to guests since it arrived last week."

"I helped arrange the athlete signings," Harris volunteers unexpectedly. "It was my agent's idea—good publicity for the Games and for the charity."

"So you signed it personally?" I ask.

"Of course," he replies, looking faintly offended. "I signed it first, actually. Got everyone else on board." He leans forward, his athletic confidence suddenly focused. "Look, why would I steal something I worked to support? That makes no sense."

"Sometimes the person with the most connection to an item is the most likely to want it," Officer Basilier observes coolly.

Harris bristles. "I have four gold medals. I don't need a wooden toy for my ego."

"Where were you yesterday afternoon around three o'clock?" I ask, keeping my tone casual.

"Training on the north slope," he answers promptly. "With my coach and about twenty other athletes. Feel free to verify."

"I was with him!" Pink Patricia chirps. "Well, not with him-with him. I was filming him from the lodge. I have it all on my channel!" She suddenly gasps dramatically. "Oh my God, I have footage from yesterday! Maybe I caught something suspicious!"

Before anyone can respond, she's swiping through her phone with alarming speed. "Here! Look!" She thrusts her phone toward Maggie, who flinches backward. "I was doing my 'Day in the Life of a Champion's Girlfriend' video yesterday. I filmed from the slopes for hours!"

Maggie hesitantly takes the phone, angling it so I can see.

The video shows Harris speeding down a slope in the distance while Pink Patricia narrates in the foreground, occasionally turning the camera to pan across the slopes where other spectators are watching.

"We should review all of your footage from yesterday," I suggest. "There might be something useful."

"I'll send everything to your tablet!" Pink Patricia says excitedly. "This is amazing content! 'The Duchess Deputizes Pink Patricia: How I Helped Solve a Royal Mystery.' We could do a collaboration video, Duchess, if you're interested—"

"She's not interested," Officer Basilier says tersely before turning her attention to Freya. "Where were you before you gave us our tour of the château, Ms. Varga?"

Freya sits up straighter. "Before you all arrived, I was in the village picking up more firewood. Several merchants saw me there between two and four. Then, I came back to the château and completed some paperwork before waiting for your arrival."

"And like I said, I was at my friend Antoine's house studying," Noah adds unhelpfully. "His mom made us hot chocolate with those little marshmallows. She can tell you I was there if you ask."

"Noah, stop interrupting," Freya shushes him. "Play your video game."

The questioning continues for another twenty minutes, with each person recounting their whereabouts during the time of the attack. Joe, meanwhile, has completed his circuit of the room and now sits beside me, occasionally eyeing Harris with what seems like suspicion.

When we've exhausted our initial questions, I stand. "Thank you all for your time. We may need to speak with each of you individually as the investigation continues."

"My channel is at your disposal, Duchess!" Pink Patricia calls as we exit the dining room. "My followers would die for an exclusive interview about the case!"

Once we're safely out of earshot in the entrance hall, Maggie lets out a long breath. "Well, that was..."

"A circus," Officer Basilier finishes flatly.

"But informative," I add. "We need to check those alibis and find that mysterious man Noah mentioned."

Maggie nods, scrolling through her tablet. "I've got a list of follow-up questions for each of them. Harris seemed defensive, don't you think?"

"Athletes usually are," I reply. "But Joe was sniffing around the room and kept eyeing Harris. I wonder if he caught a whiff of his scent? That would mean Harris was in the library."

"I'll verify as much of this as I can," Officer Basilier says, then adds, with a strange edge to her voice: "But I expect you two to handle the bulk of the interviews from here. I'm technically on vacation, after all."

I stare at her, momentarily speechless. "You're on vacation? I'm on my honeymoon!"

Officer Basilier's expression doesn't change. "Yes, but you *enjoy* this sort of thing. I've seen how you light up at a crime scene." She checks her tactical watch. "I need to do my midday security sweep anyway. Meet back here at two to compare notes?"

Before I can argue, she strides away, leaving Maggie and me standing in the entrance hall with Joe.

"Did she just..." I begin.

"Dump all the work on us while claiming she's on vacation? Yes," Maggie confirms, her fingers already typing on her tablet. "But she's not wrong about you enjoying this."

"I think something's wrong with her," I say. "Maybe Detective Freinz's comment about retirement really got to her. He broke Officer Basilier!"

"You might be right," Maggie agrees. "But we can only solve one mystery at a time."

I can't help but laugh. "Fair enough. Where should we start?"

"Kitchen staff," Maggie says decisively. "Let's find out who Noah's mystery man was."

Joe gives a soft woof of agreement, and together we head toward the château's kitchen, ready to track down a nutcracker thief.

CHAPTER
Six

THE CHÂTEAU'S kitchen is a whirlwind of activity when we push through the swinging doors. The air is heavy with the scent of butter, herbs, and freshly baked bread. Three chefs move with practiced efficiency between gleaming stainless-steel counters, calling out to each other in rapid-fire French while assistant cooks chop vegetables and stir pots. Joe's nose immediately goes into overdrive, his massive head lifting as he samples the aromatic buffet. Beside me, Maggie clutches her tablet as we navigate this culinary battleground, clearly uncertain if our investigation is welcome in the midst of lunch preparations.

A short, round-faced man in a pristine white chef's coat looks up from a sauce he's whisking and notices us. His eyes widen slightly at the sight of Joe, whose tail starts wagging hopefully at the prospect of food.

"Bonjour," the chef says, his accent thick but his smile genuine. "How may we be of service to you?"

"I'm sorry to interrupt your work," I say, stepping carefully around a young woman carrying a tray of pastries. "We're just following up on some information about yesterday's incident with Mr. Jacoby."

The chef's smile falters slightly. He sets down his whisk and wipes his hands on a towel. "Ah, yes. A terrible thing. Poor Monsieur Jacoby. Such a kind man."

"We were told someone might have been seen in the kitchen yesterday afternoon," Maggie says, tablet at the ready. "A man who doesn't work or stay here at the château."

The chef's brow furrows. "In my kitchen? Non, non. This is not possible." He turns to his staff, speaking rapidly in French. They all shake their heads, looking confused.

A tall, thin woman with salt-and-pepper hair tied back in a severe bun steps forward, wiping her hands on her apron. "Who told you this?" she asks, her accent even stronger than the chef's.

"Freya's son— Noah— mentioned seeing someone here," I explain. "Yesterday around two o'clock. A man in a hat, he said."

The kitchen staff exchange glances that I can't quite interpret. The tall woman shakes her head firmly. "Non. The boy is mistaken. No strangers in my kitchen. I would know." She taps her temple with one long finger. "I miss nothing that happens here."

Joe wanders toward a counter where a young assistant is filleting fish, his nose twitching with interest. The assistant freezes, knife in hand, looking nervously between Joe and me.

"Joe, come," I call, and to his credit, he reluctantly returns to my side, though his eyes remain fixed on the fish. "Sorry about that. He's very food-motivated."

The chef laughs, tension broken momentarily. "A dog after my own heart." He reaches into a nearby container and pulls out what appears to be a small piece of salmon. "May I?"

I nod, and he offers the morsel to Joe, who accepts it with surprising delicacy for a dog his size.

"You are sure about this man Noah claims to have seen?" Maggie presses, bringing us back to the matter at hand. "It's important."

The tall woman crosses her arms. "Perhaps the boy saw Monsieur Georges, the wine supplier? He wears a cap sometimes, delivers Tuesday afternoons."

The chef shakes his head. "Georges was not here yesterday. The delivery came Monday this week, remember? For the special dinner."

"Could Noah have been mistaken about the day?" I suggest, watching their reactions carefully.

More head shakes, more certainty that no stranger entered their domain. I exchange a glance with Maggie, whose fingers are flying across her tablet, documenting every word. Something doesn't add up. Why would Noah make up such a specific detail? And if he wasn't lying, why is the kitchen staff so adamant that he's mistaken?

Joe gives a soft whine beside me, the kind he makes when he senses something's off. I've learned to trust that sound—it's saved my life more than once during our previous investigations.

As the kitchen staff returns to their work, seemingly eager to end our conversation, a young man carrying a stack of plates pauses beside us. He's barely more than a teenager, with a smattering of acne across his cheeks and nervous eyes that dart around to make sure no one is watching him speak to us.

"Madame Duchess," he says quietly, his voice barely audible over the clatter of pots and pans. "Perhaps you should ask about the woman with the pink clothes."

I lean in, intrigued. "Pink Patricia?"

He nods quickly. "She comes to the kitchen many times. Asking questions about the château, about Monsieur Jacoby." He glances over his shoulder, then continues in an even lower voice. "She wants to know how long he has owned it, what problems it has, if he ever thinks to sell."

Maggie's eyebrows shoot up as she types this new information into her tablet. "Why would she be interested in that?" she murmurs.

The young man shrugs. "I do not know. But she films everything. Always with her phone. Even the broken pipes in the corner there." He nods toward a section of exposed plumbing near the pantry door. "Very strange to film pipes, non?"

"Very strange indeed," I agree. "Thank you for telling us."

He nods again, then jumps slightly as the chef calls his name sharply from across the kitchen. "I must go. But..." He hesitates, shifting the plates in his arms. "If you want to know more, go to *Café Chaleur, Cœurs Chaleureux* in the village. The one with the tree inside. She is there every morning, filming her videos. The owner knows everything that happens in Floconville."

With that, he hurries away, leaving Maggie and me exchanging significant looks.

"Pink Patricia investigating plumbing issues?" Maggie whispers. "That doesn't exactly scream 'content' for her travel channel."

"No, it doesn't," I agree, absently scratching Joe behind the ears as I think. "And what about Noah's mystery man? Did he see something everyone else is denying?"

Maggie taps her tablet thoughtfully. "Maybe the staff didn't see the man because they were busy elsewhere in the kitchen. Or maybe they're covering for someone?"

Joe suddenly perks up, his massive head swiveling toward the kitchen doors just before they swing open. Freya walks in, stopping short when she sees us.

If the staff were going to cover for anyone, I think, *it would be Freya.* She's earned their loyalty over many years of service.

"Oh! Rebecca, Maggie. I was just looking for you." Freya smiles, though it doesn't quite reach her eyes. "How is the investigation going?"

"We're making progress," I say, careful not to reveal too

much. "We were just following up on something Noah mentioned about seeing a stranger in the kitchen yesterday."

Freya's smile falters slightly. "Sometimes Noah has a vivid imagination," she sighs, running a hand through her hair. "I'm afraid he might have... embellished a bit to be part of the investigation. He loves his school but it's quite busy right now, and we've had some— *personal* problems— with our family." She looks at the ground as if lost in thought, then changes the subject rapidly. "Thank goodness he's been so caught up in the excitement of the Glacial Games. Harris Hastings is his absolute hero. "

I study her face, trying to determine if she genuinely believes her son made up the story or if she's covering for him for some reason. Joe, usually an excellent judge of character, seems relaxed around her, which makes me lean toward believing her.

"We're heading into the village shortly," Maggie says, tucking her tablet under her arm. "To *Café Chaleur.* Apparently it's quite the hub for local information."

"Oh, it is!" Freya's smile becomes more genuine. "Madame Fournier knows absolutely everything about everyone. And her hot chocolate is divine."

As we thank the kitchen staff and make our way out, I can't help but feel we're missing something important. Noah's mysterious man, Pink Patricia's unusual interest in the château's infrastructure, and the missing nutcracker— how do these pieces fit together?

"Well, looks like we're going for coffee after all," I say to Maggie as we head back toward the entrance hall. "Though not quite the relaxing break I had in mind."

"On the bright side, I heard their pastries are to die for," Maggie replies.

"Let's hope that's just a figure of speech," I mutter, as Joe trots ahead of us, seemingly eager for our next adventure.

The village of Floconville looks like it's been transported straight from a Christmas card as we make our way down the winding path from the château. Fresh snow crunches beneath our boots, and evergreen garlands hang from every lamppost, their red bows bright against the white landscape. Joe bounds ahead of us, leaving paw prints in the pristine snow and occasionally stopping to bury his nose in a particularly interesting drift. Maggie walks beside me, her pink hat and scarf making her look like a winter berry against the snowy backdrop, her fingers still tapping away at her tablet.

"So, Noah might be making things up, and Pink Patricia is suddenly interested in plumbing," Maggie summarizes, her breath forming little clouds in the cold air. "Neither seems like a motive for stealing a 50,000 euro nutcracker."

"Unless the nutcracker isn't the real target," I muse, watching as Joe investigates a snow-covered bush with suspicious intensity. "What if it's just a distraction?"

Maggie looks up from her tablet. "A distraction from what?"

"I don't know yet," I admit. "But why would Pink Patricia care about pipes and whether Mr. Jacoby wants to sell the château? That sounds more like real estate interest than content for her travel channel."

"Maybe she's branching out into property development?" Maggie suggests, but her tone indicates she doesn't believe it either.

We reach the edge of the village proper, where cobblestone streets have been cleared of snow but remain slick and shiny with ice. The Christmas decorations are even more elaborate here than at the château— every shop window features intricate displays, and a small carousel in the town square spins slowly, playing tinkling holiday tunes. Despite the criminal investigation that brought us here, I can't help but appreciate how perfectly festive it all is.

"There it is," Maggie says, pointing ahead to a storefront with large windows that reveal the famous tree growing through its center. "*Café Chaleur, Cœurs Chaleureux.*"

The café looks even more charming up close. The pine tree rises through the center of the round building, its trunk decorated with twinkling lights and vintage ornaments. Tables surround it in concentric circles, most of them occupied by people sipping from steaming mugs and enjoying pastries. A handwritten chalkboard outside advertises "The Best Hot Chocolate in Monrovia" and "Christmas Cookie Samplers—Limited Daily Supply."

"I can see why it's popular," I say as we approach. Joe presses close to my side as we navigate the busy sidewalk, his size causing several pedestrians to step aside with wide eyes.

We push open the café door, and a wave of warmth and the scent of chocolate, cinnamon, and pine envelops us. The café is even more magical inside— the tree's branches extend over the seating area, creating a canopy of lights and ornaments that cast twinkling patterns on the tables below. A fire crackles in a stone fireplace along one wall, and holiday music plays softly from hidden speakers.

I scan the room for the owner Madame Fournier, but before I can spot her, Joe's head swivels sharply toward a corner of the café. Following his gaze, I see a familiar figure— Pink Patricia, unmistakable in a hot pink puffer jacket and matching earmuffs, which she hasn't bothered to remove despite being indoors. She's standing beside the fireplace, phone held at arm's length, talking animatedly to the camera.

"And this, my precious followers, is the heart of Floconville's charm," she's saying, gesturing widely. "This adorable café with an actual Christmas tree growing through the building! Can you believe it, Can you believe it, mi amores? I can't! The aesthetics are absolutely breathtaking!"

Maggie and I exchange a look. "She certainly has... enthusiasm," Maggie whispers.

We make our way toward Pink Patricia, with Joe leading the charge. He seems particularly interested in her, though whether it's because he senses something suspicious or because her puffy pink jacket resembles a giant dog toy is hard to say.

Pink Patricia spots us approaching and, rather than looking concerned about being confronted by royal investigators, her face lights up. She quickly swivels her phone to capture us.

"My goodness, it's the Duchess of Atwood and her famous dog! Royal spotting alert! My followers are going to freak!" she squeals, backing up to get us in frame.

"Patricia," I begin, raising a hand to block the camera, "we need to talk to you about—"

"Call me Pink!" she interrupts. "Everyone does! Duchess Rebecca, would you mind just saying hi to my followers? They're obsessed with royalty and true crime, so this crossover moment is giving me life right now!"

"Actually," I say firmly, "we're here about the investigation. Could you put your phone down for a minute?"

Her smile falters slightly, but she recovers quickly. "Of course! Just one second—Pink Patricia signing off for now with a royal surprise guest! Don't forget to like, subscribe, and hit that notification bell!" She finally lowers the phone, though I notice she doesn't actually stop recording.

"We wanted to ask you about your interest in the château," Maggie says, tablet at the ready.

Pink Patricia finally takes a seat, settling down to sip her hot chocolate. "The château is the most picturesque Alpine retreat ever, don't you think?" She gushes, somehow making it sound like she's still filming even though she's speaking to us directly. "The rustic elegance, the history, the views—it's content gold."

"We heard you've been asking specific questions about the château's plumbing and whether Mr. Jacoby would consider selling," I say, watching her reaction carefully.

A flicker of something—annoyance? concern?—crosses her face before being replaced with her camera-ready smile. "Research, darling! My followers expect me to know everything about the places I feature. Background details add authenticity to my content."

"Broken pipes and property values seem like unusual interests for a travel vlogger," Maggie presses.

Pink Patricia laughs, the sound slightly too loud for the café setting. Several nearby patrons glance our way. "Oh, you'd be surprised what my audience finds fascinating. The last time I showed a leaky faucet in a boutique hotel in Milan, that video got two million views." She leans in conspiratorially. "People love seeing the imperfections behind the Instagram-perfect façade."

Joe moves closer to her, his nose twitching. Pink Patricia scoots her chair backward, her smile never wavering.

"What a— unique— dog!" she exclaims. "Is he always this... inquisitive?"

"Only around people who aren't being completely honest with us," I reply, holding her gaze.

Her eyes narrow almost imperceptibly, but she leans back in her chair, refusing to take the bait and engage in an argument with me. She smiles, instead. "I'm an open book, Duchess. What you see is what you get." She glances at her phone, which is still recording in her hand. "Speaking of which, I really should finish filming my café segment. The lighting is perfection right now, and my content schedule is so full..." She stands, readying to leave the cafe.

"Before you go," I say, stepping slightly to block her path, "I wanted to ask you if you saw a man walk into the kitchen the day someone attacked Mr. Jacoby?"

"If I had, I would have mentioned it," Pink Patricia chirps, her voice a tightly-lined whisper. Then her brightness returns in full force. "This has been so fun, but duty calls!" She raises her phone again, already back in performance mode. "If you'll excuse me, I have a Christmas cookie tasting to film. Hashtag holiday treats, hashtag Floconville magic!"

As she brushes past us, her pink puffer jacket makes a soft swishing sound. Joe watches her go, his amber eyes tracking her movements across the café until she exits, once again talking to her followers on her livestream. A bell above the door clanks behind her, offering a note of finality.

"She's hiding something," Maggie says quietly, tapping notes into her tablet.

"Definitely," I agree. "But what? And how does it connect to the nutcracker?"

Joe gives a low woof of agreement, still staring at the seat where Pink Patricia recently perched.

Maggie nods in agreement, and we quickly ask the barista if the owner is at the shop today. The barista tells us she's away, enjoying the start of the Glacial Games.

"This visit is a bust," Maggie whispers to me, frustration shaking her braids.

"Don't worry," I say, thinking about what we've learned. "We're on the right track. We just need a nose like Joe's to help us through the snow."

CHAPTER

Seven

LATER IN THE EVENING, Jack and I find a moment to have a real honeymoon.

We're alone. No Maggie updating us on waffle sizes, no Officer Basilier scanning for assassins behind the potted plants, no Pink Patricia filming our every move. Just me, my husband, our dogs, and a meal that smells divine enough to make Joe whimper hopefully from his spot by the fire.

The château's private dining room glows with firelight, casting dancing shadows across antique furniture and our faces as Jack raises his wine glass to mine. Outside, snowflakes swirl against the darkness like confetti in slow motion, but in here, everything is warm, intimate, and for once, blessedly free of our entourage.

"To my beautiful wife," Jack says, his eyes reflecting the golden flicker of flames. "And to finally getting a moment alone on our honeymoon."

"I'll drink to that," I reply, clinking my glass against his. The wine is rich and velvety, a selection from Mr. Jacoby's personal collection. Even with a bandaged head, he insisted on choosing the perfect bottle for our "private dinner à deux," as he called it.

Joe and Luma are sprawled on a plush rug near the hearth, forming an unlikely pair— one a golden mountain of fur, the other a sleek, elegant silhouette. Despite their differences, they've developed an easy companionship that mirrors our own. Luma's head rests on Joe's massive paw, her eyes half-closed in contentment.

Jack follows my gaze to our dogs and smiles. "They have the right idea. Relaxing by the fire, not a care in the world."

"No stolen nutcrackers in dog world," I agree, taking another sip of wine.

"Speaking of which..." Jack begins, but I hold up a hand to stop him.

"Can we save the investigation talk for dessert, at least? For now, I just want to be Rebecca, your wife, not Rebecca the Duchess Detective."

Jack's smile softens. "Of course. I do expect a full briefing over crème brûlée." He reaches across the small table and takes my hand, his thumb tracing gentle circles on my palm. "How about we talk about something more pleasant instead? Like our future."

"Our future?" I echo, raising an eyebrow. "We've been married less than a month. Isn't it a bit soon to be planning our retirement?"

"Well, we *are* in our fifties," Jack says, his tone light but with an undercurrent I can't quite place. "Have you ever thought about what comes next? After Castle Atwood, the Royal obligations, all of it?"

I study his face, noticing the slight tension around his eyes despite his casual demeanor. "Occasionally," I admit. "But I hardly saw *this* plot twist coming, so I thought... why bother planning? I assumed I'd signed up for a lifetime of curtseying and ribbon-cutting when I married you."

"What if I told you I've been thinking about stepping away from it all? Not immediately," he adds quickly, seeing my surprise. "But someday. Finding a place of our own, away from the pomp and circumstance. A property in the country-side, perhaps. Room for the dogs to run. Privacy. Normalcy. We could run our own foundation for causes we care about."

I set down my wine glass slowly, processing his words. "You want to leave royal life? Can you even do that?"

"I'm third in line," Jack says with a small shrug. "My Aunt's first-born son— my cousin— is in his late fifties and fully intends to take the throne. His daughter— my first cousin once removed— is second in line, but only sixteen years old. She has time to grow into the role. As third in line, little is expected of me."

"Family trees confuse me," I say, my head suddenly hurting. "You're third in line because…"

"My father was the Queen's brother, before he passed," Jack says sadly. "When the Queen had her own child, and then *he* had his own child, my place in line was, thankfully— bumped down. A fact I'm very grateful for. The chances of me ever taking the throne are slim to none. And the truth is..." He hesitates, looking momentarily vulnerable in a way he rarely allows himself. "I'm tired, Rebecca. The constant scrutiny, the expectations, the rules— it wears on me more than I usually admit."

Our dinner arrives before I can respond, making Jack's point— a young staff member wheels in a cart with covered dishes. He serves us with quiet efficiency, but can't help sneaking a glance at Jack before he places the dishes down. Steaming plates of coq au vin appear before us, along with sides of roasted vegetables and crusty bread. The rich aroma of wine-braised chicken fills the air, momentarily distracting Joe from his fireside nap. His head lifts, nose twitching with interest.

"No," I tell him firmly, though I know Jack will sneak him a piece when he thinks I'm not looking.

We wait for the staffer to wheel out his tray, and the man seems to take his time. He glances at us sheepishly before exiting. Once we're alone again, I return to our conversation, carefully considering my response. "I didn't realize you felt that way about royal life," I say softly. "You've always seemed so... at ease with it all."

Jack cuts into his chicken, steam rising from the tender meat. "Years of practice. The Duke of Atwood performing his role perfectly." He smiles, but it doesn't quite reach his eyes. "Don't get me wrong— I understand my privilege, and I value the good we can do with our position. But sometimes I dream of something simpler."

"Tell me about this country property of yours," I say, genuinely curious about this side of Jack I haven't fully seen before.

His face transforms as he describes it, animation replacing the weariness I'd glimpsed moments before. "Nothing ostentatious. A farmhouse, perhaps, with land around it. Somewhere in the Monrovian countryside, where the hills roll on forever and the nearest neighbor is just a dot on the horizon. A place where Joe and Luma could run free without security following their every move." He takes a bite of food, chewing thoughtfully before continuing. "Maybe some horses. A vegetable garden. Books—lots of books. Perhaps I could even work at the local library."

"It sounds lovely," I say, picturing the scene he's painting. "Though I'd miss Maggie's organizational skills. I haven't done my own laundry in months."

Jack laughs, the sound warm and genuine. "I'm sure we could figure it out. There must be instructional videos online."

"Oh God, we'd be asking Pink Patricia for household tips."

We both chuckle at the thought, and I feel a tightness in my chest I hadn't realized was there begin to loosen. The idea of a future beyond Castle Atwood isn't something I've allowed myself to consider much. The transition from San Diego animal trainer to Monrovian Duchess has been overwhelming enough without planning the next chapter.

"What would you do?" Jack asks, breaking into my thoughts. "In this hypothetical country retreat of ours?"

I don't even have to think about it. "I'd open an exotic animal sanctuary," I say immediately. "Take in all those creatures that people buy as status symbols then abandon when they realize a tiger cub grows into an actual tiger." I warm to the idea as I speak. "And I'd keep solving mysteries on the side, of course. The Duchess Detective becomes the Countryside Crime-Solver."

"Of course," Jack says with a fond smile. "Perhaps Maggie would want to join you and live nearby, so you wouldn't have to be without your best friend. I can see it now—you, Joe, and Maggie tracking down the Case of the Missing Mail Order Bride, or the Mystery of the Vanishing Veterinarian. "

"Hey, country crimes can be just as interesting as castle murders," I protest, pointing my fork at him playfully. "And it would be a nice change of pace to investigate something that doesn't involve royalty or priceless artifacts."

"Like stolen nutcrackers?" Jack raises an eyebrow.

"You said we'd save that for dessert," I remind him.

"So I did." He takes another sip of wine, his expression becoming more serious. "You know, I've never told anyone else about wanting to step away someday. Not even my family. They wouldn't understand— they see our position as an unquestionable privilege, not something anyone would willingly relinquish."

"What changed?" I ask. "Why tell me now?"

Jack's eyes meet mine across the table. "Because it's not just *my* future now. It's ours."

We finish our main course in comfortable silence, the only sounds the crackling of the fire and the occasional contented sigh from Joe or Luma. When the staff returns to clear our plates and bring dessert—the promised crème brûlée, served with fresh berries— Jack leans back in his chair with a satisfied expression.

"Alright, Detective Duchess," he says. "Dessert has arrived. Time for that briefing you promised me."

I tap the caramelized sugar topping with my spoon, enjoying the satisfying crack before scooping up a bite. "Where to begin? It's been quite a day of sleuthing."

As I fill Jack in on the details of the case, I can't help but think about how lucky I am: I've chosen a man who always puts me first. And I may not have found him until a little later in life than some others might have expected; but sitting here, now— I know that life is full of adventures, and you only have to look around the next corner with open eyes to find them.

THE NEXT MORNING, the château's lobby takes my breath away. Light streams through the château's stained-glass windows, painting the marble floor in jewel-toned patterns that even Joe finds fascinating. He sniffs at a vibrant blue spot near his paw as I yawn, still feeling the effects of last night's wine and late conversation with Jack. Our private dinner feels like a distant dream already, the peaceful bubble of "just us" popped by the reality of our entourage gathered by the hotel's entrance. Everyone is bundled in winter gear and looking expectantly at Maggie, who's clutching her tablet with a familiar gleam in her eye that means she's planned something.

"There you are!" Maggie calls, waving enthusiastically as Jack and I approach with our dogs in tow. "We've been waiting for you!"

I'm about to apologize for our tardiness when I notice something so shocking that I actually stop mid-stride.

"Officer Basilier?" I ask, blinking rapidly to make sure I'm not hallucinating. "Is that you?"

The woman standing beside Maggie is technically Officer Basilier— same height, same sharp eyes constantly scanning for threats— but everything else about her has undergone a transformation so complete it borders on the supernatural. Her usually severe hair has been styled into short, soft waves that frame her face. Her tactical gear has been replaced by a fashionable ski outfit in deep burgundy. But most shocking of all are her fingernails, painted a cheerful holiday red with tiny snowflakes on each one.

"Good morning, Duchess," she says, actually smiling. "Beautiful day for outdoor activities, isn't it?"

I exchange a bewildered look with Jack, who seems equally stunned.

"Did you... get a makeover?" I ask, unable to stop myself.

She laughs—actually *laughs*—and holds up her decorated nails. "The château has a lovely spa in the basement level. I had the full treatment last night— facial, manicure, and the most amazing hot stone massage. Marie has magical hands, I swear."

"Marie?" Jack mouths to me silently, eyebrows raised to his hairline.

"I've just decided to take it a little easier," Officer Basilier says, rambling. "I mean, I'm not ready to retire yet, and none of *you* think I should retire—"

We all shake our heads, offering a chorus of "of course nots!" and "you've got plenty left to do!" It's out of friendly support, but also because Officer Basilier is shooting us a look that says "you better agree I'll use my taser."

"— so I just decided to treat myself! I'm on vacation," she continues. "And even though crime never sleeps, maybe I've been taking it all too seriously. Maybe I *need* a more relaxed life. Orange is a Duchess, but maybe *I* could treat myself like a Princess!" There's a manic look in her eye that says she's been thinking about this all night.

Before I can process this alternate-universe version of Officer Basilier, Freya bustles into the lobby carrying a tray of steaming to-go cups. Her cheeks are flushed from the cold, and snowflakes cling to her hair like tiny diamonds.

"Perfect timing!" she says, smiling at Jack and me. "I thought everyone might enjoy these before heading out. They're cinnamon nutmeg lattes—our chef's specialty."

She distributes the cups with efficient grace, even placing a small dish of whipped cream on the floor for Joe and Luma. "Just a little treat," she says when she catches my surprised look. "Mr. Jacoby insists all guests receive equal hospitality, including the four-legged ones."

Joe doesn't wait for permission, his massive tongue making the whipped cream disappear in one enthusiastic lick. Luma, ever the proper royal pet, waits for Jack's nod before daintily sampling her portion.

"This is delicious," I say after taking a sip. The latte is perfectly spiced, with just enough sweetness to balance the espresso bite. "Please thank your chef for us."

"I will," Freya replies. "And Mr. Jacoby asked me to check if there's anything else you need before I head back to help him with some paperwork. He's feeling much better this morning."

"We're all set, thank you," Jack says warmly.

With a quick smile and a small curtsy that she cuts short—remembering our preference for informality— Freya disappears back into the depths of the château.

"So," I say, turning to Officer Basilier and gesturing at her entire appearance. "This is vacation mode, huh? I didn't know you had one."

Officer Basilier shrugs elegantly. "The Duchess and you seem to have it well in hand. I'm officially declaring myself on vacation duty." She raises her cup in a mock toast. "To delegating."

Benjamin, who's been unusually quiet, finally pipes up. "Does this mean you're coming to the Glacial Games with us, then? Just as a spectator?"

"The Glacial Games?" I repeat, looking from Benjamin to Maggie.

"That's what I was about to announce when you came in!" Maggie practically bounces on her toes with excitement. "Given the nature of our investigation, I explained to Mr. Jacoby that we might need to speak with Harris Hastings at the competition, and he gave us all tickets for today's events!"

She pulls a fan of glossy tickets from her coat pocket, displaying them proudly like winning lottery numbers. "Front row access to all the preliminary events—skiing, snowboarding, ice skating. The whole works!"

Benjamin's eyes light up like a child on Christmas morning. "We're going to see the Glacial Games live? With actual athletes? This is better than Indiana Jones and the Last Crusade!"

Jack laughs, accepting the ticket Maggie hands him. "I haven't been to the Games in years. My cousin competed in the junior division when we were teenagers."

"I didn't know you were interested in winter sports," I say, taking my own ticket.

"There's still a lot we're learning about each other," Jack replies with a wink that makes my stomach do a little flip. "I'm actually quite knowledgeable about skiing. I used to go every winter with my father."

Benjamin looks at Jack with newfound respect. "Your Grace, perhaps you could explain some of the technical aspects to me? I've only seen skiing in American movies."

"I'd be happy to," Jack says, clapping Benjamin on the shoulder.

"Rebecca, I know you're not much for sports," Maggie says, offering me my ticket. "But I thought this would be a chance to, you know... *investigate.*" She whispers the last word as if she's committing a crime.

Not much for sports is understatement, I think. I've hated sports my entire life. But finding a nutcracker requires sacrifices, so I tuck the ticket in my bag.

Maggie hands the last ticket to Officer Basilier, who tucks it into her designer ski jacket with a satisfied nod.

"Perfect timing for my vacation declaration," she says. "I'll enjoy watching the events while you two—" she points at Maggie and me, "—interrogate suspects and chase down clues."

"We don't interrogate," Maggie protests. "We interview."

"Semantics," Officer Basilier waves dismissively, then checks her watch. "We should leave soon if we want good seats. The first events start in an hour."

As everyone gathers their belongings and prepares to head out, I take a moment to appreciate the absurdity of our situation. My honeymoon has transformed into a group outing to a sporting event where we'll be investigating an Olympic-level athlete for potential theft and assault. Joe nudges my hand with his nose, as if sensing my thoughts.

"What do you think, buddy?" I whisper to him. "Think we'll find our nutcracker thief at the Glacial Games?"

He gives a soft woof that I choose to interpret as confirmation.

"The dogs are coming too, right?" Benjamin asks, already holding Luma's leash while she sits patiently at his feet.

"Absolutely," Jack confirms. "Joe's investigative skills might come in handy."

"And Luma loves the snow," Benjamin adds, looking down at Jack's collie with affection. "Don't you, girl?"

Luma responds with a dignified tail wag that makes Joe look like an uncoordinated teenager by comparison.

As we file toward the entrance, Maggie falls into step beside me, lowering her voice. "I've been doing some research on Harris Hastings," she says. "Did you know he's retiring after these Games? He hasn't announced it publicly, but my sources say this is his last competition."

"Interesting timing," I murmur, my investigator instincts immediately perking up. "Right when he's staying at the château where a valuable item connected to the Games goes missing."

"My thoughts exactly," Maggie nods, her expression turning serious despite her excited tone earlier. "Pink Patricia has been strangely absent this morning too. No live streaming, no ambush interviews."

"Let's keep our eyes open at the Games," I say. "Harris might reveal something useful when he's in his element."

Maggie nods, already typing notes into her tablet as we step out into the bright mountain morning, the snow crunching beneath our boots. The sky is a perfect blue, and the air feels like breathing in winter itself—crisp, clean, and exhilarating. Despite the circumstances, I can't help but feel a flutter of excitement. A day at the Glacial Games with my husband, my dog, and yes, even our eclectic entourage, sounds like exactly the honeymoon adventure I never knew I wanted.

Plus, if Harris Hastings is our thief, I'm going to enjoy watching him sweat—figuratively and literally—as we close in on him.

———

The Glacial Games venue sprawls across the mountainside. Enormous viewing stands ring multiple competition areas, each one packed with spectators bundled in colorful winter gear. Flags representing countries from around Europe snap in the mountain breeze, and the buzz of excited conversations in multiple languages creates a soundtrack to match the visual spectacle. As our group makes our way through the main entrance, I can't help but feel a twinge of gratitude for Maggie's efforts— our tickets allow us to bypass the enormous line stretching down the mountain path.

"This is magnificent," Jack says beside me, his eyes sweeping across the venue with genuine appreciation. "They've expanded since I was last here. The half-pipe for the snowboarders is twice the size it used to be."

"Half-pipe?" Benjamin repeats, looking confused. "Like plumbing?"

"It's what they call the U-shaped snow structure the snowboarders use for tricks," Jack explains patiently. "We should watch some of the competitions there—the athletes get incredible air."

"I want to see that," Officer Basilier announces, surprising us all again with her enthusiasm. She's scanning the venue map with the same intensity she usually reserves for security threats. "The snowboarding competition starts in twenty minutes on the north side."

I exchange a bemused glance with Jack. "I didn't realize you were a snowboarding fan, Officer."

She actually looks slightly embarrassed. "I used to date a snowboarder. Before I joined the force." She tucks a strand of her newly styled hair behind her ear. "I find the technical aspects fascinating."

"Technical aspects," Maggie repeats with a knowing smile. "Sure."

"The male competitors are quite skilled," Officer Basilier adds, a hint of defensiveness in her tone.

"I bet they are," I say, suppressing a laugh.

Officer Basilier checks her watch. "I'm going to secure a good viewing position," she announces, already moving toward the north side of the venue. "Enjoy your... investigating."

We watch her weave through the crowd with the same purposeful stride she usually employs when scanning for assassins, only now her target appears to be attractive men on snowboards.

"I'm not sure I'll ever get used to vacation mode Basilier," I mutter to Maggie.

"I kind of like her," Maggie replies. "Though I'm documenting everything for future leverage."

Benjamin turns to Jack, practically bouncing with excitement. "Your Grace, shall we go see the skiers? The program says Harris Hastings will be doing practice runs at the east slope."

"Good idea," Jack agrees. "We can take Luma with us—she loves running in the snow." He turns to me, lowering his voice. "Unless you'd prefer I stay with you for the investigation?"

I shake my head. "Go enjoy the sports with Benjamin. Maggie, Joe, and I can handle Harris."

"Are you sure?" Jack asks, a hint of concern in his eyes.

"Positive," I assure him. "Besides, Joe is worth at least three human security guards."

As if to confirm this, Joe gives a confident woof, his amber eyes alert as he surveys the crowds around us.

"Alright, then," Jack says, leaning in to kiss me quickly. "We'll meet back at the central lodge for lunch? Say, one o'clock?"

"Perfect," I agree.

Jack and Benjamin head off toward the east slope with Luma trotting elegantly between them, her sleek collie form drawing admiring glances from passersby.

"Just like old times," Maggie says cheerfully, consulting her tablet. "The three of us on the case."

"You, me, and Joe," I agree, patting my dog's massive head. "The dream team."

We make our way through the crowd toward the media area, where Maggie's research indicates Harris Hastings should be giving interviews. Joe stays close to my side, occasionally growling softly when someone pushes too close to us. His size creates a natural buffer that most people instinctively respect.

"There he is," Maggie whispers, pointing ahead to where a small crowd of reporters surrounds a tall figure in a sleek racing suit emblazoned with sponsor logos. Harris Hastings stands with perfect posture, his dark hair falling artfully over one eye just like in his posters, speaking confidently into a cluster of microphones.

Pink Patricia hovers at the edge of the media scrum, phone held high as she films everything. Her outfit today is, predictably, pink from head to toe, though she's added a white fur trim to her hat and jacket that makes her look like a fashion-forward Mrs. Claus.

We position ourselves close enough to hear Harris's interview but far enough away that we don't appear to be eavesdropping. Joe sits at my feet, his eyes fixed on Harris with the intensity he usually reserves for steak dinners.

"Mr. Hastings," one of the reporters asks, "how does it feel coming into these Games as the defending champion? Is there extra pressure?"

Harris flashes his camera-ready smile. "The only pressure I feel is the pressure I put on myself to perform at my best. This competition is particularly important to me personally."

"Why is that?" another reporter calls out.

Harris's expression shifts subtly, something almost melancholic passing across his features before the professional smile returns. "Let's just say I want to make sure I leave everything on the mountain. If the worst should happen and this is my last game, I want to make sure it's an epic one for the fans."

The reporters immediately erupt with questions, but Harris holds up a hand. "That's all for now, folks. I need to prepare for my practice run."

Pink Patricia pushes forward as the other reporters begin to disperse. "Harris, baby! Just one quote for my followers about what makes the Château des Flocons special for your pre-competition preparation!"

He gives her a tight smile that doesn't reach his eyes. He shoots Patricia a knowing look, then whispers, "Not now, Patricia."

As Harris steps away from the media area, Maggie nudges me. "Now's our chance."

We intercept Harris before he can reach the athlete-only section, with Joe positioning himself strategically to block any quick escape.

"Mr. Hastings," I say, stepping into his path. "I was hoping we could speak with you briefly."

He stops, recognition flickering in his eyes. "Duchess," he says with a slight nod that falls short of the respect my title usually commands. "I'm afraid I'm on a tight schedule."

"This will only take a moment," I assure him. "We were interested in what you meant during your interview just now. About the off chance this could be your last game?"

His jaw tightens almost imperceptibly. "I was speaking hypothetically. Every athlete knows any competition could be their last. Injuries happen."

"That's not what it sounded like," Maggie interjects, her tablet ready to record any important details. "It sounded more... definitive."

"Well, you misinterpreted," Harris says curtly. "Now if you'll excuse me, I have a practice run scheduled."

"We also had a couple more questions about the nutcracker," I say directly, watching his reaction.

Something flashes in his eyes—anger? Fear? It's gone too quickly to identify. "I already told you. I signed the nutcracker, like all the other athletes. Why would I steal it?" He glances at his watch with exaggerated impatience. "I really must go."

"Of course," I say, stepping aside. "We wouldn't want to

interfere with your preparation for what *might* be your final competition."

His eyes narrow slightly at my emphasis, but he says nothing more before striding away, his posture rigid with tension.

"Well, that was interesting," Maggie says once he's out of earshot.

"Very," I agree. "He let something slip in that interview. He's not ready to publicly announce his retirement yet, but that comment he made about never knowing what competition could be your last was strange."

"He was defensive about the nutcracker," Maggie adds.

Joe gives a low whuff, which I've come to interpret as his agreement. The scent of something delicious distracts him, though, his nose lifting to sample the air.

"I smell it too," I tell him, spotting a food cart nearby with a small crowd gathered around it. "Let's regroup and discuss over a snack."

The cart is selling aebleskivers— round Danish pancakes served hot and filled with jam. Steam rises from the cooking pan where an elderly woman expertly flips the spherical treats with a special tool. We order a dozen, plus an extra plain one for Joe, and find a relatively quiet spot near a decorative pine tree to enjoy our spoils.

"Harris was definitely hiding something," I say, biting into an aebleskiver filled with raspberry jam. The warm, fluffy pancake practically melts in my mouth.

Maggie nods, thumbing through something on her tablet while balancing her food in her other hand. "I've been doing more research on him. I wanted to tell you in the hotel lobby this morning but there were too many people around." Maggie glances over her shoulder to make sure no one is listening. "My digging shows he's had financial troubles recently. One of his major sponsors dropped him last year after a poor performance. It was in the tabloids. Zacharia emailed me a copy. "

"Really?" I toss Joe his plain aebleskiver, which he catches mid-air with surprising delicacy for a dog his size. "How bad are these financial troubles?"

"Bad enough that he's been selling some of his properties," Maggie says, showing me the article on her tablet. "Including a vacation home in Switzerland that went for well below market value last month."

I frown, connecting dots in my mind. "So Harris Hastings is potentially retiring, has money problems, and was distinctly uncomfortable talking about the stolen nutcracker."

"Which is worth 50,000 euros," Maggie adds, popping another aebleskiver into her mouth.

"Still, that doesn't seem like a lot of money to someone like Harris, does it?" I ask. "And then there's Pink Patricia, asking around about plumbing in the château. Do you think they're working together?"

Maggie's eyes widen. "Maybe? But I can't believe either one of them would hurt Mr. Jacoby. And why target something Harris helped support for charity?"

I shake my head, offering Joe another aebleskiver as a reward for his patience. "I'm not sure yet. But I'm starting to think the nutcracker might be connected to something bigger. Something that involves the château itself."

As we finish our snack, I watch Harris in the distance, preparing for his practice run. Despite his celebrity status and athletic grace, there's something almost desperate in his movements now that I'm looking for it. Like a man performing not just for the crowd, but for his own survival.

"Let's keep digging," I tell Maggie. "I have a feeling Harris Hastings has more secrets than just retirement plans."

CHAPTER
Nine

AFTER WANDERING around the Glacial Games on our own for another hour, we find the rest of our group waiting at the central lodge— though I barely recognize Officer Basilier at first glance. She's transformed from tactical security professional to enthusiastic tourist with astonishing completeness. Her arms are laden with shopping bags, a fuzzy pompom hat is perched on her head, and what appears to be a commemorative Glacial Games scarf wraps around her neck. Joe immediately recognizes Jack and Luma, trotting ahead of me and Maggie with his tail wagging so vigorously his entire back end sways from side to side.

"There you are!" Jack calls out, his smile warming me despite the mountain chill. Luma sits primly at his feet, her tail sweeping a small arc in the snow when she spots Joe.

"Officer Basilier?" I ask, unable to hide my amazement as I approach. "Did you rob the gift shop?"

She beams at me—actually *beams*—and holds up a shopping bag emblazoned with the Glacial Games logo. "Souvenirs! I got one for everyone at the station. And look!" She lifts one foot, showcasing a pair of gleaming new snow boots with what appears to be custom Monrovian crests on the sides. "Limited edition. Only fifty pairs made."

Maggie leans close to me, whispering, "Who is this woman and what has she done with our Officer Basilier?"

"I heard that," Officer Basilier says without losing her smile. "And I'll have you know, I might never come back to the police force. Do you realize there's an entire world of people who don't have to check for assassins under every table? It's liberating!"

Benjamin, who's been fiddling with a disposable camera, looks up with wide eyes. "You're quitting? But who will protect us from international espionage?"

"Don't be ridiculous," she replies, though there's no bite in her tone. "I'm simply considering my options. Life is short, and there are so many specialized snow boots I haven't worn yet."

I exchange a glance with Jack, who shrugs as if to say, "Just go with it."

"Listen, Officer Basilier," I begin, stepping closer. "Maggie and I just spoke with Harris Hastings, and he was acting extremely suspicious. When we mentioned the nutcracker—"

She holds up a hand, cutting me off. "Nope! Not today. I'm sure it was very suspicious and very exciting, but I'm on vacation, remember?" She adjusts her new hat. "You two are Royal Investigators. You've got this. When you need someone arrested, I'll be there with handcuffs. Until then, I'm going to enjoy watching extremely fit athletes perform impressive physical feats."

"But—" Maggie tries, clutching her tablet.

"But nothing," Officer Basilier interrupts cheerfully. "I have complete faith in your abilities. You two have wanted to investigate on your own for quite some time, and now I suppose you can—"

"That's not true—" Maggie starts to say, but Officer Basilier interjects.

"Now, where's that hot chocolate stand I saw earlier?"

As Officer Basilier scans the crowd, Jack moves to my side, his hand finding mine. "While you two were detective-ing, Benjamin and I saw something you should know about."

"We saw him," Benjamin says dramatically, lowering his voice to a stage whisper. "The detective with the attitude. He's here."

"Detective Freinz?" I ask, feeling Joe press against my leg at the mention of the name.

Jack nods. "He was lurking near the officials' tent, looking like he was up to something. We thought you should know."

"He definitely wouldn't like you poking around," Benjamin adds. "He has that look, you know? Like the bad guy in every action movie ever. All he needs is a scar across his eye and a white cat to stroke while he explains his evil plan."

Despite the seriousness of the situation, I can't help but smile at Benjamin's description. "We'll keep an eye out for him. Thanks for the warning."

"If you ask me," Jack says, "his presence here means something in and of itself. Maybe he has a lead on the case and he's at the Glacial Games to investigate?"

"Or he's a sports fan?" Maggie suggests weakly.

Benjamin shakes his head. "Men like that don't enjoy things. They just... brood and plot."

"Speaking of plotting," Officer Basilier says, returning her attention to us, "shouldn't we head to our seats? Harris Hastings' event starts in twenty minutes."

"About that," Jack says, a small smile playing at his lips. "I've got a surprise. Mr. Jacoby didn't just give us regular tickets."

He leads us through the crowded venue, past regular seating areas and up several flights of stairs. Joe stays close to my side, occasionally casting longing glances at food vendors we pass. Finally, we reach a private entrance where an attendant checks our tickets and nods respectfully.

"Right this way, Your Grace," he says, leading us through a corridor that opens into a spacious private box with plush seating, a small buffet table, and a perfect view of the ski slopes where Harris will be competing.

"This is incredible!" Maggie gasps, rushing to the glass front of the box. "We can see everything from here! Mr. Jacoby really did us a solid."

The box is heated to a comfortable temperature, allowing us to remove our heavy outer layers. Luma immediately finds a cushioned spot near the window, curling up with a perfect view of the slopes. Joe remains standing, his nose twitching with interest as he surveys our luxurious surroundings.

"There's even champagne," Benjamin notes, pointing to an ice bucket on the side table.

"And those little sandwich things without crusts!" Officer Basilier adds, already helping herself.

I move to the window, taking in the spectacular view of the mountain course. Athletes are doing practice runs, colorful blurs against the pristine white snow. The stands below are filling with spectators, a sea of winter hats and scarves moving like waves.

My stomach chooses this moment to growl audibly, reminding me that aebleskivers, while delicious, weren't exactly substantial. The aroma wafting up from a vendor directly below our box doesn't help.

"I smell pretzels," I say, my mouth watering. "Real German ones, with the thick salt crystals."

Jack comes to stand beside me, following my gaze to the pretzel vendor. "Want one? I could use a snack myself."

"I want one too!" Benjamin chimes in. "And Maggie probably does, and Officer Basilier..."

"Everyone wants pretzels," Maggie confirms, not looking

up from her tablet where she's undoubtedly documenting our Harris Hastings encounter.

Jack shrugs. "I'll go with Rebecca to get them. We can bring back enough for everyone."

"I'll watch Luma," Benjamin offers, already sitting down beside the collie.

Joe gives a sharp bark, his entire body suddenly alert.

"Yes, Joe, you can come too," I laugh, interpreting his enthusiasm correctly. "I know how you feel about pretzels."

Officer Basilier frowns slightly. "Your Grace, is it wise for you and the Duchess to go without security?"

Jack raises an eyebrow. "I thought you were on vacation?"

She hesitates, clearly torn between her professional instincts and her newfound leisure persona. Finally, she glances down at her new boots. "These are giving me blisters anyway. I should probably stay off my feet for a bit." It's clear there's a deep conflict within Officer Basilier— a Freudian clash of two sides of the self.

"We'll be fine," I assure her. "Nobody even recognizes Jack with his hood up, and we'll have Joe with us. He's better than any security detail."

"Besides," Jack adds with a small smile just for me, "we could use a few minutes of privacy on our honeymoon."

Officer Basilier rolls her eyes, but there's no real annoyance behind it. "Fine, but don't blame me if you get mobbed by pretzel-seeking fans."

"We'll be back before Harris competes," I promise, already heading for the door with Joe at my heels, eager for both the promised pretzel and a rare moment alone with Jack amidst our chaotic honeymoon adventure.

———

The venue buzzes with excitement as we make our way down from the private box, Joe trotting faithfully beside us with his nose twitching at each new food scent we pass. Jack keeps his hood pulled low over his face, and I'm struck by how different it feels to move through a crowd with him when he's not being recognized as royalty. No one stops us, no one stares— we're just another couple at the Glacial Games, heading for pretzels with their oversized dog.

"This is nice," Jack says, his gloved hand finding mine as we navigate the crowded concourse. "Just being people instead of titles."

Joe leads the way, his massive frame creating a natural path through the throng of spectators. He seems to know exactly where we're going, his nose unerringly guiding us toward the pretzel stand I spotted from the box.

The line isn't as long as I expected, though the aroma of freshly baked dough and melted butter has attracted a steady stream of customers. We join the queue, and Jack wraps his arm around my shoulders, pulling me close against the mountain chill.

"Benjamin will want extra salt on his," I muse, mentally tallying our pretzel order. "And Maggie likes hers with mustard."

"And Officer Basilier?" Jack asks with a grin.

"Probably something hyper-specific we don't even know exists," I reply. "Artisanal pretzel with imported Himalayan pink salt and truffle-infused cheese dip."

Jack laughs, the sound vibrating through his chest against my shoulder. "You're terrible," he whispers, but his eyes sparkle with amusement.

When we reach the front of the line, we order six large pretzels with various toppings. Joe sits patiently at my feet, his eyes never leaving the vendor's hands as he wraps our order. I can practically see the longing in my dog's amber gaze.

"And one plain one for the dog," Jack adds, noticing Joe's fixation. "No salt."

"Big fellow," the vendor comments with an appreciative nod toward Joe. "Looks like he could eat the whole stand."

"He'd certainly try if we let him," I agree.

Pretzels secured in a cardboard tray, we step away from the stand. Before we can head back toward the stairs, Jack suddenly tugs me into a shadowed alcove between two souvenir shops. Joe follows, looking momentarily confused by the detour.

"Jack, what—"

He cuts me off by pressing his lips to mine, his free hand cupping my face with unexpected tenderness. I melt into the kiss, careful not to tip over the pretzel tray balanced in my other hand. When he pulls away, his eyes are bright with an almost boyish delight.

"I've been wanting to do that all day," he says, his voice low. "It's just so nice being able to kiss my wife without someone taking our picture or Officer Basilier clearing her throat disapprovingly."

"I'm not complaining," I murmur, leaning in for another quick kiss. "Though if we don't head back soon, they'll send a search party."

"Let them," Jack grins, but he steps back, taking the pretzel tray from me. "Alright, back to our regularly scheduled honeymoon-slash-investigation."

We emerge from our moment of privacy and head toward the stairs that lead back up to the private boxes. Joe trots ahead, his pretzel still securely wrapped and held in Jack's free hand. The stairs are steep and numerous, winding up the side of the stadium seating. We've only climbed a few steps when Joe suddenly freezes, his ears perking forward. He makes a soft sound in his throat—not quite a growl, but a warning.

I touch Jack's arm, stopping him mid-step. "Joe hears something."

My dog turns his head toward the space beneath the stairwell— a shadowed area partially concealed by a decorative event banner. I strain my ears and catch the sound of voices— angry, tense voices that seem jarringly out of place amidst the festival atmosphere.

"—don't care what you believe, Detective," comes a familiar voice— Mr. Jacoby's distinctive accent, though his usual warmth is replaced with barely contained fury. "These accusations are preposterous."

Jack and I exchange a glance. Silently, we step off the stairs and move closer to the banner, positioning ourselves where we can hear but remain unseen. Joe stays by my side, his body tense and alert. We peer over the edge of the banister, where the cutout beneath the stadium lies. The space beneath the steps is cold and angular, its concrete bones exposed and draped with festival detritus— discarded food wrappers, confetti, a forgotten knit glove. Within its clutches, Detective Freinz and Mr. Jacoby stand almost chest-to-chest, a tableau caught in a shaft of pale winter light leaking through the slats. Jacoby's hands are balled at his sides—a trembling that reads as both fear and fury—while Freinz's stance is pure predatory stillness. The detective's wool coat bulks his silhouette, but it's the eyes that give away his animosity: cold, fixed on Jacoby's face with a steely patience.

Neither man notices us, though Joe hunkers low, ears flat, the hair on his shoulders bristling. He knows a fight when he sees one. Jack's fingers find mine and squeeze, our small, silent contract to keep still and listen.

"I told you already, I have nothing to say to you," Jacoby hisses. His accent is sharper now, all the vowels clipped. "If you have a problem with my business, you take it to the proper channels. I don't answer to you."

Freinz's voice is so gravelly it sounds like a threat even when he's asking a question. "You want the proper channels? Fine. I'll drag your name through every one of them until there's nothing left for you to lord over." He leans in, lowering his voice. "The historical society is just one vote away from removing the castle from your grasp forever. And given your involvement with the latest unsavory event there—"

"*My* involvement?" Jacoby exclaims. "That's preposterous!"

"Preposterous? I don't think so." Detective Freinz's gravel-rough voice drips with contempt. "It's the perfect scheme, isn't it? Stage a theft, fake an injury, file an insurance claim. You thought you'd get to keep your precious château and pocket a nice sum for your 'medical expenses.' Not on my watch"

"That's absurd!" Mr. Jacoby sputters. "I was genuinely attacked. What kind of man do you think I am?"

"The desperate kind," Detective Freinz replies coolly. "Your château is falling apart. The plumbing alone needs a complete overhaul that you can't afford. It's a blight on the town and an insult to our history. Stealing the nutcracker kills two birds with one stone—insurance money plus a sympathy wave that might increase bookings. But I won't allow you to keep that castle."

I feel Jack stiffen beside me, his hand tightening around the pretzel tray. Joe's lip curls slightly, revealing the edge of a fang. I place a calming hand on his head, silently urging him to stay quiet.

"I won't let you intimidate me..." Mr. Jacoby's voice breaks slightly. "The château is my home. It belongs in my family."

"It *belongs* to who the people of Floconville charter with its care," Detective Freinz cuts in. "We both know Château des Flocons should be in better hands. My brother's offer still stands— perhaps with a slight adjustment downward, given recent... incidents."

There's a rustling sound, followed by Mr. Jacoby's voice, now steel-hard with conviction. "I've told you both a hundred times—the château is not for sale. Not to him, not to anyone."

"Perhaps you'll feel differently, when I've built a case against you for insurance fraud, It will be," Detective Freinz says, his voice lowering to something truly menacing. "One way or another, the château will change hands. I'll make sure of it."

"Are you threatening me, Detective?"

"I'm stating facts."

Joe shifts restlessly at my side, and a pretzel wrapper crinkles too loudly in Jack's hand. We freeze, holding our breath.

"What was that?" Detective Freinz's voice sharpens.

Jack tugs my arm, gesturing with his head away from the banister. Without a word, we back away quietly, moving as quickly as we dare without making noise. Joe follows, understanding the need for stealth.

Once we're a safe distance up the stairs, we quicken our pace and disappear into the crowd, climbing rapidly with our pretzel bounty still mostly intact.

"We need to tell the others," Jack whispers urgently. "This changes everything."

"Detective Freinz practically admitted his brother is behind this," I agree, my mind racing. "They're trying to force Mr. Jacoby to sell the château."

Joe looks up at us, his expression as serious as a dog's can be. I scratch behind his ears briefly as we climb.

"Good boy for staying quiet," I tell him. "Though I almost wish you'd bitten the detective."

"That would have complicated our investigation," Jack points out, though I can see in his eyes he's not entirely opposed to the idea.

We reach the top of the stairs, slightly out of breath from our hasty retreat. Before we reenter the private box, Jack pauses, his face serious.

"Rebecca, this is dangerous. If Detective Freinz is willing to threaten Mr. Jacoby so openly..."

"Then he won't hesitate to cause problems for anyone who gets in his way," I finish, understanding his concern.

Jack nods grimly. "So much for our peaceful honeymoon."

"To be fair," I say with a small smile, "we never actually expected one, did we?"

With a deep breath and pretzels in hand, we push open the door to rejoin our friends, ready to share what we've discovered beneath the stairs.

CHAPTER
Ten

"YOU'RE KIDDING," Maggie says, her pretzel frozen midway to her mouth as Jack and I finish recounting what we overheard beneath the stairs. Her eyes are wide with disbelief, a smudge of mustard clinging to her lip. "Detective Freinz actually threatened Mr. Jacoby? Right here at the Games? That's... that's criminal intimidation!"

Joe, finally enjoying his well-earned pretzel beside me, gives a low woof of agreement. I scratch behind his ears absently while scanning our private box to make sure we're not being overheard. Benjamin looks appropriately horrified, while Officer Basilier has momentarily shed her vacation persona, her eyes narrowed in professional assessment.

"It was pretty blatant," Jack confirms, settling back into his seat beside me. "Detective Freinz is trying to force Mr. Jacoby to sell the château."

"And he implied that the theft and attack might just be the beginning of 'unfortunate incidents' if Mr. Jacoby doesn't cooperate," I add, the memory of the detective's menacing tone still fresh in my mind.

Officer Basilier sets her pretzel down with military precision. "That crosses every ethical line in law enforcement. If what you heard is accurate, this is grounds for an internal affairs investigation."

"It's more than unethical," I say. "It's a motive. And to top it off, Detective Freinz is accusing Mr. Jacoby of staging the attack to collect insurance money."

Maggie takes a bite of her pretzel, chewing thoughtfully before shaking her head. "That's ridiculous. Mr. Jacoby would never fake his own attack. He's a Lord! He has standards."

I raise an eyebrow at her. "Being a Lord guarantees good behavior? Need I remind you about that Duke we investigated last spring who was stealing his own family's jewelry to fund his gambling habit?"

"Or my second cousin twice removed who faked his own kidnapping to get out of a royal wedding?" Jack adds dryly.

Maggie sighs. "Fair point. But Mr. Jacoby just seems so... genuine. When he talks about the château, you can tell it means everything to him."

"I agree," I say, watching Joe lick pretzel salt from his paws. Luma appears beside him and joins in, disguising getting the last crumbs of salt off his feet as a kind cleaning gesture. "I don't think Mr. Jacoby faked anything. It's just more intimidation. Detective Freinz is trying to frame him to force the sale."

Benjamin, who's been quietly listening while feeding tiny bits of his pretzel to Luma, suddenly perks up. "This might sound crazy but... Is it possible Detective Freinz stole the nutcracker and attacked Mr. Jacoby?"

"Or hired someone to do it?" Jack suggests.

"I've thought the same," I say. "But the Detective wasn't staying at the château. He didn't have a clear opportunity to attack. And there's something that doesn't add up about Harris and Pink Patricia..."

Maggie's fingers fly across her tablet screen. "I've been doing more research on Harris. His financial troubles are worse than I initially thought. His last major sponsor dropped him six months ago, and he's been liquidating assets ever since."

"Desperate people do desperate things," Officer Basilier murmurs, her vacation demeanor completely gone now.

A sudden fanfare of trumpets interrupts our conversation, drawing our attention to the slopes below. The announcer's voice booms through the stadium, reverberating off the mountains: "Ladies and gentlemen, the men's freestyle skiing competition is about to begin!"

The crowd roars in response, a wave of sound that washes over us even in our private box. Down on the slopes, officials in bright orange jackets make final preparations while cameras pan across the spectators, occasionally displaying faces on the massive screens positioned around the venue.

"We'll continue this discussion after the competition," Jack says, settling more comfortably in his seat. "For now, let's not draw attention to ourselves. Detective Freinz might be watching."

I nod, though my mind continues to race with theories and connections. Joe seems to sense my distraction, pressing his warm body against my leg in silent support. I give him another scratch behind the ears, grateful for his steadfast presence.

The first competitor takes his position at the top of the slope, a tiny figure against the vast expanse of white. The announcer introduces him with flourish— a Swiss champion with multiple medals to his name. Even from our distance, I can see the intensity in his posture as he readies himself.

"And he's off!" the announcer calls as the skier pushes forward, rapidly gathering speed as he descends the mountain.

The crowd gasps collectively as he launches into his first aerial maneuver, spinning and twisting with impossible grace before landing perfectly. Even I, with my limited knowledge of winter sports, can appreciate the skill involved.

"Triple cork 1620," Jack explains beside me, his eyes tracking the skier's movements. "Extremely difficult. He rotated four and a half times while doing three off-axis flips."

"Show-off," I tease, nudging him with my shoulder.

"I told you I know skiing," he replies with a grin that still makes my heart skip.

We watch as three more competitors tackle the course, each attempting to outdo the last with increasingly complex aerial stunts. The crowd responds with appropriate awe, the excitement building with each performance.

"Harris Hastings is up next," Maggie announces, checking the program on her tablet. "He's the favorite to win, according to all the betting predictions."

Sure enough, the announcement comes: "Next on the course, representing Monrovia, four-time champion Harris Hastings!"

The crowd erupts in wild cheering as Harris appears at the top of the mountain, his sleek racing suit gleaming in the sun. Even from this distance, there's no mistaking his confident stance and artfully tousled dark hair. The camera zooms in on his face, projecting it onto the giant screens— his expression is focused, intense, with none of the celebrity charm he displays in interviews.

"He looks different," I murmur to Jack. "More... determined."

"It's his last competition," Jack reminds me. "Even if he hasn't announced it publicly yet. That's a lot of pressure."

I scan the stands, spotting Pink Patricia in a nearby VIP box, her bright pink outfit impossible to miss. She's filming with her ever-present phone, bouncing slightly with excitement. But there's something off about her enthusiasm— it seems forced, almost theatrical.

"The judges give the signal," the announcer calls, "and Harris Hastings begins his run!"

Harris pushes off, his form perfect as he builds speed

down the slope. The crowd falls into an expectant hush, all eyes tracking his progress. Even Joe has lifted his head, seemingly captivated by the human flying down the mountain.

"He's going for something big," Jack says, leaning forward.

Harris hits the first jump, soaring into the air with spectacular height. He twists and flips with machine-like precision, landing smoothly before immediately building speed for the next feature. The crowd roars its approval.

"That was flawless," Benjamin whispers in awe.

Harris approaches the middle section of the course— a series of rails and smaller jumps designed to showcase technical skill. He navigates them with fluid ease, barely seeming to touch the features before he's moving to the next. It's like watching a dancer who happens to be on skis.

"The final jump is coming up," Jack says, his voice tense with anticipation. "This is where he'll attempt his signature move— the one that won him the gold last time."

I find myself holding my breath as Harris rockets toward the massive jump. Time seems to slow as he leaves the ground, launching higher than any previous competitor. His body contorts into the first rotation, arms tucked tight against his chest, skis perfectly parallel.

And then— a slight wobble. So small that I might have missed it if I weren't watching so intently.

"Uh-oh," Jack says sharply, half-rising from his seat.

Harris's rotation falters mid-air. His arms fly out, desperately seeking balance where there is none to find. The crowd's collective gasp is like a physical force, pressing against my ears as we all witness the moment where control is lost.

He hits the landing wrong, his weight off-center. One ski catches an edge, violently twisting his leg. The other ski detaches completely, flying off into the snow like a projectile. Harris's body tumbles, ragdoll-like, across the slope in a sickening series of impacts.

"Oh my God," Maggie whispers, her hand covering her mouth.

A scream pierces the stunned silence— Pink Patricia, on her feet in the nearby box, her phone forgotten as she reaches out uselessly toward the crumpled form on the snow. The sound is primal, raw with terror.

Harris lies motionless on the slope, one leg bent at an uncomfortable angle. Medical staff are already rushing toward him, their orange jackets bright against the white snow. The crowd remains in shocked silence, the only sound the urgent shouts of the emergency personnel.

"That was planned," Officer Basilier says suddenly, her voice low and certain.

Shock ripples through our group. Maggie drops her pretzel.

"That's a horrible thing to say!"

I tear my eyes away from the terrible scene below to see if Officer Basilier's joking. It's clear: she's serious. "How would someone plan a fall like that?!" I exclaim.

Officer Basilier's face is set in hard lines, all traces of her vacation persona gone. "I used to date a competitive snowboarder, remember? I know what equipment failure looks like." She points to the screen, which is replaying the accident in slow motion. "Watch his right binding—the one that released. It gives way before he loses control, not after."

Jack leans forward, his eyes narrowed. "She's right. His ski detaches too early. That's not normal failure."

A cold feeling settles in my stomach as I watch the replay again. The binding does indeed release before Harris's body begins to twist, not as a result of the fall.

"Are you saying someone tampered with his equipment?" I ask, though I already know the answer.

Officer Basilier nods grimly. "That's exactly what I'm saying."

"But who would—" Benjamin begins, then stops as understanding dawns on his face. "Oh. The nutcracker thief? But why?"

Down on the slope, Harris is being carefully secured to a backboard, medical staff working with practiced efficiency. Pink Patricia has disappeared from her box, presumably rushing to be with him. The announcer's voice, subdued now, informs the crowd that the competition is temporarily suspended.

"This changes everything," Jack says quietly. "If someone tried to hurt Harris..."

"Then the nutcracker theft might be connected to something much bigger than we thought," I finish for him.

Joe presses against my leg, sensing my distress. I place a hand on his warm head, drawing comfort from his solid presence as my mind races through the implications. Harris Hastings's financial troubles, Pink Patricia's strange questions about the château, Detective Freinz's threats to Mr. Jacoby, and now a potentially deliberate equipment failure that could have killed a champion skier.

"I think we need to talk to Pink Patricia," I say finally. "Right now, before anyone has a chance to get to her."

"She'll be with Harris," Maggie points out. "At the medical tent."

I stand, decision made. "Then that's where we're going." I look at Officer Basilier. "Still on vacation?"

She rises, so eager to help she almost knocks over her chair. "Of course, Orange. Officer reporting for duty." Then, she pauses, clearing her throat and taking on the aura of someone who doesn't care. "I mean, I suppose I can spare a moment from shopping to help." She shrugs casually, then adds, "Not that I'm bored! I love being on vacation. "

As our group gathers to leave, I cast one last glance at the slope where Harris fell. The snow compresses where his limp form just lay, a stark reminder of what's at stake. Someone was willing to risk a man's life today.

And I intend to find out who.

CHAPTER
Eleven

THE MEDICAL TENT LOOMS AHEAD, white canvas walls snapping in the mountain wind while urgent voices leak through the seams. My boots crunch across trampled snow mixed with dirt, but I try to silence the soft crunching sound. I'm eavesdropping— trespassing where I shouldn't be.

Joe presses against my leg as we approach the entrance, his usual enthusiasm dampened by the smell of antiseptic and fear that wafts from within. Even from outside, I can hear Pink Patricia's voice, high and frantic, demanding to know if Harris will ever ski again. The medical staff's responses are measured, professional, deliberately vague.

"Jack, you and Benjamin should wait out here with the dogs," I say, turning to my husband. "Too many people will just complicate things."

Jack nods, understanding immediately. "We'll keep watch. If Detective Freinz shows up—"

"He will," Officer Basilier interrupts, her vacation persona temporarily abandoned. "A man like him can't stay away from the chance to watch a man he hates suffer."

Benjamin shifts nervously, gripping Luma's leash. "Should we warn you somehow if we see him coming?"

"Just cough loudly," Maggie suggests, already edging toward the tent flap. "We'll hear it."

I give Joe a quick scratch behind the ears before following Maggie and Officer Basilier into the tent. The transition from bright mountain sunshine to filtered canvas light makes me blink, and the smell hits me full force— that particular cocktail of disinfectant, sweat, and barely controlled panic that every medical facility shares.

Harris lies on a stretcher in the center of the space, his right leg immobilized in a temporary splint that makes my stomach turn just looking at it. At first glance, Harris's injury doesn't seem catastrophic. His pant leg has been cut away, the skin beneath puffy and angry but intact, and the way his boot dangles from the stretcher says 'torn ligament' more than 'life-changing trauma.' For a split second I even feel a tiny flutter of relief— this is bad, but not the kind of bad to upend a man's future.

Harris's face, usually camera-ready with that practiced celebrity charm, is gray and drawn, sweat beading on his forehead despite the cold. Pink Patricia hovers beside him, mascara streaking down her cheeks in parallel black rivers, her phone nowhere in sight for possibly the first time since I've met her.

"Harris," she's saying, gripping his hand so tightly her knuckles are white, "you're going to be fine. The best doctors in Europe will fix this. You'll ski again, I know you will."

Harris's eyes are glazed, probably from whatever pain medication they've given him, but I catch the flicker of something—disagreement? resignation?— when she mentions skiing again.

A medic in a red jacket looks up as we enter, his expression shifting from professional concern to annoyance. "This is a restricted area. Family only."

"We're investigators," Officer Basilier says, flashing her badge with an authority that makes the medic step back.

"We need to speak with Mr. Hastings about what happened."

"He's in no condition—" the medic begins, but Harris's voice, rough and strained, cuts him off.

"It's fine." He tries to shift on the stretcher and winces. "Let them... let them ask."

Well, that's a change, I think, surprised that Harris is agreeing to speak with us. *Maybe he hit his head, too.*

Maggie and I move closer, careful not to crowd Pink Patricia, who looks at us with suspicion.

"Harris," I begin gently, "we need to know if you noticed anything unusual about your equipment before the run. Any tampering, anyone near your skis who shouldn't have been there?"

His eyes struggle to focus on me. "I... I don't..." He swallows hard, and Pink Patricia quickly offers him water from a plastic cup. "Everything seemed normal. I checked my bindings myself, like always."

"But Officer Basilier noticed the binding released before you lost control," Maggie presses, tablet ready. "She saw it in the replay video. That's not normal."

Harris's brow furrows, the effort of remembering clearly painful. "There was... someone was in the equipment area. Before my run. But everyone's always there, coaches, techs, other skiers..."

Before he can continue, the tent flap flies open with such force that Pink Patricia jumps, nearly dropping the water cup. Detective Freinz strides in like he owns the place, his dark uniform making him look like a storm cloud in human form. His eyes sweep the tent, landing on us with obvious displeasure.

"Out," he barks at us. "This is a police investigation now."

"We have every right—" Officer Basilier begins, but Freinz cuts her off with a look that could freeze antifreeze.

"Your jurisdiction ended about three hundred miles ago,

Officer. This is my investigation, my witness." He jerks his head toward the exit. "Out. Now."

"You can make them leave, but not me," Officer Basilier says, nodding and Maggie and me. She offers us a wink and we take the hint, exiting the tent. Before we leave, I notice that Harris has gone even paler at Freinz's arrival. He looks nervous, as if he's a suspect in his own accident. Maggie catches my eye and tilts her head slightly toward the tent wall. The two of us exit the tent, but we don't go far. Instead, we position ourselves just outside, close enough to the thin canvas walls that we can hear everything.

"Mr. Hastings," Freinz's gravel voice carries easily through the fabric, "I need you to think very carefully. Did you see anyone tamper with your skis?"

There's a pause, then Harris's weak voice: "I told the ladies, everyone was in the equipment area. It's chaos before events."

"Everyone," Freinz repeats, his tone suggesting he finds this unhelpful. "Be more specific. Who specifically did you see near your equipment?"

"My coach, obviously. Pink— Patricia was there filming. Some of the Norwegian team..." Harris trails off, then adds, "Wait. There was someone else."

My pulse quickens. Beside me, Maggie has her ear practically pressed against the tent wall.

"Who?" Freinz demands.

Before Harris can answer, another voice joins the conversation— warm, concerned, and completely unexpected.

"Excuse me, I'm sorry to interrupt."

Mr. Jacoby. I recognize his refined accent immediately.

"I heard about poor Harris's accident," Mr. Jacoby continues. I risk a peek through an opening in the tent and confirm it's him, sporting his favorite plaid vest. There's a sad look in his eyes. Mr. Jacoby is a genuinely kind man, as far as I can tell. "I brought him some tea," he continues. "It's a special blend from the château, very soothing. We want all of our guests in good health."

There's rustling, the sound of liquid sloshing in a cup, then Pink Patricia's voice: "That's very kind of you, Mr. Jacoby."

"Think nothing of it, my dear. Harris is a guest of the château, after all. His wellbeing is my responsibility."

"Actually," Detective Freinz's voice drops to something almost predatory, "your presence here is fortuitous, Lord Jacoby. Mr. Hastings was just about to tell us who he saw near his equipment."

A pause stretches like pulled taffy, thick with tension. Then Harris speaks, his voice stronger now, carrying clearly through the tent wall.

"It was him."

My breath catches. Maggie grabs my arm. I peek through the tent opening again just in time to see Harris's arm still raised in the air, pointing straight at... *Mr. Jacoby.*

"And you're certain?" Freinz presses.

Harris drops his arm, and I duck back behind the opening in the tent, my heart pounding.

"It was Mr. Jacoby," Harris continues. "I saw Mr. Jacoby in the skiers' chalet, near the equipment. Just minutes before my run."

The silence that follows is deafening. Even Pink Patricia seems to have lost her voice.

"That's... that's absurd!" Mr. Jacoby finally sputters. "I was nowhere near the equipment area. I was watching from the stands!"

"This is insane!" Mr. Jacoby protests. "I would never— I couldn't— Harris, you must be mistaken! I was nowhere near the tent..."

"Yes, you were," Pink Patricia says carefully, her voice flush with a dawning realization. "I was interviewing the players, but Harris mentioned he saw you in the equipment area. You dropped off gift bags, didn't you? For the players, from the château?"

"Those were left in the tent yesterday!" Mr. Jacoby protests. "Freya dropped them off. I wasn't anywhere near the tent."

"Detective Freinz!" Officer Basilier objects. "You can't be considering such circumstantial evidence..."

"Harris," Detective Freinz continues, ignoring Officer Basilier. "Are you saying Mr. Jacoby tampered with your skis?"

"I'm saying I saw him there," Harris responds weakly, his voice barely a mumble. "Near my skis. And then... and then they failed. It doesn't mean he did it but—"

"But he's lying about his presence there," Detective Freinz's voice has gone official, formal. "Mr. Jacoby," he continues, "I'm placing you under arrest for the attempted murder of Harris Hastings, as well as suspected insurance fraud in connection with the theft of the nutcracker and your own alleged attack."

"This is outrageous!" Mr. Jacoby shouts.

"Stop this at once!" Officer Basilier calls out. "As a fellow law enforcement officer, I must object!"

But the sounds of struggle, of handcuffs clicking, tell me Detective Freinz isn't interested in protests. Maggie and I look at each other, our faces mirrors of disbelief: Mr. Jacoby has just been arrested.

"Mr. Jacoby's had a very bad week," she whispers, and despite everything, I almost laugh at the understatement.

———

We step away from the medical tent— acting as if we've been investigating a nearby crepe stand— just as Detective Freinz emerges with Mr. Jacoby in handcuffs. I have to look away from the older man's stricken face— it's like watching someone's entire world crumble. The crowd parts for them, phones appearing like mushrooms after rain as people capture the spectacle of a Lord being arrested at the Glacial Games. Mr. Jacoby keeps his chin up, maintaining what dignity he can, but his plaid vest looks suddenly shabby against the metal restraints.

"This is wrong," Maggie says beside me, her fingers flying across her tablet as she documents everything. "All of it. The timing, the accusation, everything."

Officer Basilier joins us, shaking her head. "There was nothing I could do," she says, her face pained as she watches Freinz march his prisoner toward a police vehicle. "Freinz is enjoying this too much. Look at his posture— shoulders back, chin lifted. He's performing for the crowd."

We make our way back to where Jack and Benjamin wait with the dogs. Joe spots me first, his tail creating a small snowstorm as he wags it enthusiastically. But even his greeting feels subdued, as if he senses the wrongness of what just happened. Luma sits perfectly still beside Jack, her elegant head tilted as she watches the crowd's reaction to Mr. Jacoby's arrest.

"That bad?" Jack asks, reading my expression before I can speak.

"Worse," I tell him, but before I can elaborate, I notice we have company. Freya stands beside Benjamin, looking oddly out of place in her practical winter coat among all the ski fashion. Noah is with her, wearing a snowboarding outfit that looks slightly too small for him, like he's grown since it was purchased but refuses to admit it doesn't fit.

"Rebecca!" Freya greets me with genuine warmth, though there's tension around her eyes. "We didn't expect to see you here."

She doesn't know yet, I think, pained that we'll have to be the ones to break the news of Mr. Jacoby's arrest to Freya.

"Freya was just telling me they came to watch the Games,"

Jack explains, his hand finding mine in that automatic way that still makes my heart skip. "Noah's quite the winter sports enthusiast, apparently."

Noah doesn't look up from his phone, but his cheeks flush slightly at the attention. He's got that particular teenage awkwardness where every mention of his existence seems to cause physical pain.

"It's his favorite event of the year," Freya says, ruffling her son's hair despite his attempt to duck away. "We save up specially for tickets. Don't we, Noah?"

The boy mumbles something that might be agreement, his eyes still glued to his screen. But I notice he keeps glancing toward the police vehicle where Mr. Jacoby is being loaded into the back seat.

"Is that… ?" Noah starts to ask, his eyes wide as he recognizes Mr. Jacoby in the Police cruiser.

Before Noah can continue, I jump in: "Freya," I begin carefully, not sure how to break this news, "something's happened. This is difficult to share, but… Mr. Jacoby was just arrested for the attempted murder of Harris Hastings."

The color drains from her face so quickly I'm afraid she might faint. "Arrested? But… he couldn't have! He *wouldn't* have…"

"Detective Freinz is accusing him of faking his own injury, stealing the nutcracker, and—" I pause, watching her grip Noah's shoulder for support, "—and tampering with Harris Hastings' skis. Harris identified him as being near the equipment just before his run."

"No." The word comes out as a whisper, then stronger: "No, that's impossible. Mr. Jacoby isn't capable of such things. He's the kindest man I know. He would never hurt anyone, let alone a guest of the château!"

Noah has gone rigid beside his mother, his phone forgotten in his hand. His face has taken on a grayish cast that makes me think of spoiled milk.

"Mom," he says, his voice cracking in that way teenage boys' voices do when they're stressed, "does this mean we're definitely going to have to move now?"

The question hangs in the air like a missed ski jump, suspended in that moment before the inevitable crash. Freya's face flushes deep red, and she looks at us with the expression of someone whose private struggles have just been laid bare for public consumption.

"Noah, this isn't the time—"

"But you said if anything else bad happened at the château, we'd have to leave!" His voice rises, drawing stares from passing spectators. "You said we couldn't afford to stay if Mr. Jacoby had to sell! And Mr. Jacoby didn't do anything! I *know* he didn't! This is all wrong!" There's a certainty in Noah's voice that makes me pause. I'm not sure why his tone strikes me as important, but I file the information away for later.

"Noah, I won't do this with you here!"

"Yes, you have to!" Noah says, tears leaking from his eyes. "You won't talk to me about anything and I want to know right now!" He lets out a choked sob. "The château is my home!" Noah's voice cracks again, tears threatening at the corners of his eyes. "All my friends are here! Antoine's here! I don't want to go to some stupid public school in some stupid other town! And Mr. Jacoby didn't do anything! He's my friend, too."

"Noah, please—"

"No!" He jerks away from his mother's hand. "This isn't fair! First Dad leaves, then he stops sending money, now Mr. Jacoby's arrested and we have to move? I hate this! I hate everything!"

Before anyone can respond, he takes off running, his too-small snowboard jacket flapping as he pushes through the crowd. Freya's face crumples for just a moment before she pulls herself together.

Freya closes her eyes briefly, and when she opens them, there's a resignation there that breaks my heart a little. "I'm sorry," she says to us, her voice quiet but steady. "Noah's right. We've been... struggling. His father—" She pauses, clearly weighing how much to share. "His father runs a gambling operation outside of town. It's not... it's not going well. He hasn't sent money in months. I've been trying to make it work on my salary alone," Freya continues. "But Noah's school is expensive. I have to—" she wipes her own eyes, clearly trying to pull herself together. "I have to go after him. If you'll excuse me..."

She doesn't wait for our response, but hurries after her son, calling his name as she disappears into the crowd of Glacial Games spectators. We stand there in a small circle of awkward silence, even Joe and Luma seeming unsure how to react to the emotional outburst.

"That," Benjamin finally says, "was a very, very upset kid."

"Can you blame him?" Jack asks quietly. "His whole world is falling apart."

I watch the spot where Noah disappeared, thinking about the desperation in his voice, the raw fear of losing everything familiar. There's something about his reaction that niggles at me, some connection my brain is trying to make but can't quite reach.

"Did anyone else think his reaction was... intense?" I ask, looking around our group. "Even for a upset teenager?"

Maggie nods slowly, already typing notes. "He seemed almost personally offended by Mr. Jacoby's arrest. Like it was aimed at him specifically."

"These things are hard on kids," Officer Basilier observes, though her investigator's instincts are clearly engaged. "They often internalize blame, think everything is connected to them somehow."

But I can't shake the feeling that there's more to Noah's outburst than teenage angst. The way he mentioned the château, his father's gambling troubles, the timing of everything...

Joe nudges my hand with his wet nose, pulling me from my thoughts. His amber eyes seem to ask what I'm thinking, and I wish I had a clear answer for him.

"We should head back to the château," I say finally. "There's nothing more we can do here, and frankly, I've had enough of the Glacial Games for one day."

As we gather ourselves to leave, I cast one last look at the medical tent, then at the police vehicle disappearing down the mountain road with Mr. Jacoby inside. Something about this whole situation feels orchestrated, like we're watching a play where everyone knows their lines except us.

"You're thinking Detective Freinz set this whole thing up," Jack says quietly, reading my expression with his usual accuracy.

"I'm thinking someone did," I reply, taking his offered arm as we begin walking toward the venue exit. "The question is whether Freinz is the puppet master or just another puppet."

Joe walks beside us, his massive head low, occasionally sniffing at the snow as if he might find answers there. And maybe he will—after all, he's solved cases before that had us humans completely stumped.

CHAPTER
Twelve

THE IMPOSING Floconville jail looks like it belongs in a fairy tale— but the Brothers Grimm kind where people lose fingers, not the Disney version. It's a squat, stone building with narrow windows centered around a wooden door built hundreds of years ago. The dull gray cinderblocks of the prison's exterior are patched with lichen and centuries-old graffiti, some of it too worn to read. Steps lead up the jail's wooden door, iron bands holding warped pieces of wood together.

Joe's nails click against the worn cobblestones as we approach, his massive head swiveling to take in the outdated prison. *This place is bad news,* his eyes seem to say. Maggie clears her throat, her braids swinging with determination as we prepare to request a meeting with Mr. Jacoby.

"I can't believe they're actually keeping him here," Maggie whispers as we reach the heavy wooden door. "It's like something out of the Crusades. Do they even have proper cells? What's for dinner… gruel?"

"I guess we're about to find out," I say, pushing open the door that groans in protest.

The interior of the jail is as unsettling as its exterior. A single desk sits at the front, manned by an officer who looks about twelve but probably just has good genes. Behind him, I can see a narrow hallway leading to what I assume are the cells— all three of them, if the small size of this building is any indication.

"Excuse me," I say, stepping forward. "I'm Rebecca Orange, the Duchess of Atwood. My colleagues and I would like to speak with Mr. Jacoby, please."

The young officer looks up from his paperwork, his eyes widening as he takes in my presence, then Maggie's, then finally landing on Joe with visible alarm.

"Your Grace," he stammers, rising quickly to his feet. "We weren't expecting... that is to say, Detective Freinz left strict instructions that Mr. Jacoby isn't to have visitors."

"I'm sure he did," I reply, channeling every ounce of duchess-ness I can muster. It still feels like wearing someone else's clothes, but I'm getting better at the performance. I try to copy Jack's "Duke voice,"— the one I've heard him use in moments where he needs to project authority. "However, as representatives of the Royal Investigators Office, we have jurisdiction that supersedes local police in matters concerning Monrovian nobility."

Beside me, Maggie casually pulls up something on her tablet and turns it to face the officer. "Royal Declaration 1873, Paragraph 4, Subsection B," she says with the confidence of someone who definitely didn't just Google this information five minutes ago.

The officer frowns, clearly torn between Detective Freinz's orders and the royal authority we're wielding with what I hope is convincing authenticity.

"And the dog?" he asks, eyeing Joe with trepidation.

"Royal service animal," I say without missing a beat. "He's trained to detect certain chemical compounds that might be relevant to our investigation."

This is, of course, complete nonsense. Joe's only training is to sit for treats and not chase the castle giraffe, but the officer doesn't need to know that.

After a moment's hesitation, he nods. "Very well, Your Grace. Please follow me."

He leads us down the narrow hallway to the cells, which are as medieval as I feared— stone walls, iron bars, and wooden benches built to torture. Only one cell is occupied, and Mr. Jacoby sits there looking utterly out of place in his plaid vest and bandaged head. He's reading a small paperback book that he quickly sets aside when he hears us approach.

"Visitors for you, sir," the officer announces, then turns to us. "You have fifteen minutes."

As he retreats back to his desk, Mr. Jacoby rises to his feet with the dignified air of someone receiving guests in his drawing room rather than a jail cell.

"Duchess Rebecca, Ms. Lefevere, and the magnificent Joe," he says, his voice steady despite the circumstances. "What an unexpected pleasure!" He sounds like he's about to offer us tea, but then looks around as if it's only just hit him he doesn't have a teapot.

"Mr. Jacoby," I begin, stepping closer to the bars. "We wanted to check on you and ask you some questions about what happened."

Joe approaches the cell carefully, his nose working overtime as he sniffs the air. After a moment's consideration, he sits beside me, his expression alert but not alarmed. I take this as a good sign— Joe's instincts about people have proven remarkably accurate in the past.

"I appreciate your concern," Mr. Jacoby says, his eyes briefly lingering on the bandage wrapped around his head. "As you can see, I'm being treated to the finest accommodations Floconville has to offer." His attempt at humor falls flat, the strain around his eyes betraying his true feelings. There's fear in his expression, and the moment makes me want to hug him.

"We know you didn't do this," Maggie says firmly, her tablet already poised for note-taking. "Harris's identification of you at the equipment area seems... convenient."

"Extremely convenient for Detective Freinz," Mr. Jacoby agrees, his expression darkening. "I was nowhere near the skier's equipment. I was in the stands the entire time, as dozens of witnesses could attest if the Detective bothered to interview them."

"Do you have any enemies, Lord Jacoby?" I ask, getting straight to the point.

"Please, please," he waves a hand in the air. "It's *Mr.* Jacoby, not Lord. I hate to use titles. You might understand why, Duchess," he smiles at me, then motions at his surroundings. "I've come to learn that titles don't protect you from the worst of life, or promise you the best things, either. Better to ignore them all together, don't you think?"

"I understand," I say, nodding. "Mr. Jacoby, do you know who might have wanted to frame you? Can you think of any reason Harris would lie about your presence?"

He gives a short, humorless laugh. "Other than a bribe from Detective Freinz himself? I can't imagine why Harris would lie. I've always tried to be fair in my business dealings and kind in my personal ones."

He pauses, running a hand through his thinning hair. "But apparently, owning a historic château makes one more enemies than friends."

"Tell us about your past with Detective Freinz," I prompt, watching his reaction carefully. "We overheard him threatening you at the Games, but how long has this been going on?"

Mr. Jacoby sighs, lowering himself back onto the uncomfortable-looking bench. "Years. It started with minor harassment— excessive building inspections, noise complaints about guests, that sort of thing. But in the last year, it's escalated." He leans forward, lowering his voice. "His brother, Albert Freinz, is a real estate investor. Or more accurately, a real estate vulture. He swoops in where properties are distressed and flips them for profit."

"And he wants the château," Maggie says, typing rapidly on her tablet.

"Desperately," Mr. Jacoby confirms. "He's made multiple offers, each one more insulting than the last. When I refused, the Detective began finding 'violations' at the château— plumbing issues, electrical concerns, structural problems that mysteriously appeared right before inspections. He's gone to the historical society as well to try to invoke some ancient law that allows the people to reclaim land from the monarchy. It's a good law, all in all," Mr. Jacoby says, scratching his chin. "I support the idea that the public should control our historical lands. But even good laws can be put to poor use by those who wish to use them for personal gain."

Joe shifts beside me, a low rumble in his chest that isn't quite a growl but definitely indicates disapproval. I scratch behind his ears absently, my mind piecing together the pattern.

"So Detective Freinz is using his position to pressure you into selling to his brother," I say. "But why escalate to framing you for theft and attempted murder?"

Mr. Jacoby's shoulders slump slightly. "The historical society was beginning to question his repeated citations. Several members visited the château last month and found it 'charming' despite the Detective's claims of imminent collapse." A small smile touches his lips. "The Detective needs something more dramatic to force my hand—something that would make the town turn against me."

"Like framing you for stealing a valuable nutcracker, insurance fraud, and attacking a beloved athlete," Maggie concludes.

"Perhaps," Mr. Jacoby nods. "And he's not the only one. Everyone seems to want my château these days, even though it's a money pit. The plumbing is from another century, the electrical work needs constant attention, and the roof—" He waves a hand dismissively. "But people see only the façade, the romance of owning a piece of history. They think they can turn it into a gold mine without understanding the work involved."

I exchange a glance with Maggie. "You mentioned 'everyone.' Have there been other offers besides Detective Freinz's brother?"

Mr. Jacoby's eyebrows rise in surprise. "Oh yes, several. Just last week, in fact, I received an anonymous offer through a shell company." He shakes his head in disbelief. "Significantly above market value, which was suspicious enough, but still less than what the property is worth to me sentimentally."

"Do you remember the name of the company?" Maggie asks, her fingers hovering over her tablet.

"Of course. It was rather absurd— Pink Express, I believe. Very modern-sounding for such an old property."

Maggie's fingers freeze above her screen, her eyes meeting mine with a significant look. *Pink Patricia.* It has to be.

"Pink Express," Maggie repeats, typing it into her notes with deliberate precision. "And you declined this offer?"

"Naturally," Mr. Jacoby says. "As I said, the château isn't for sale at any price. It's been in my family for generations, and I intend to keep it that way." He pauses, a shadow crossing his face. "Or at least, I did before all this."

Joe leans against my leg, sensing my heightened interest. I scratch his head, grateful for his steady presence as I consider this new information.

"Mr. Jacoby," I say carefully, "we ran into Freya and Noah at the Games yesterday. They seemed... upset about the possibility of having to move if you sell the château."

Pain flickers across his face, quickly masked but unmistakable. "Ah, yes. I imagine they would be." He sighs heavily. "Freya has been with me for almost a decade now. She's more than an employee— she's family. And Noah... that boy has had such a difficult time."

"His father," I prompt gently.

Mr. Jacoby's expression hardens. "A worthless gambler who abandoned them years ago, yet still manages to cause pain from a distance." He shakes his head in disgust. "He's always promising Noah money for school trips or new clothes, then failing to deliver because he lost it all at the tables. Freya works so hard to make up for his shortcomings, taking on extra shifts, saving every penny." His voice softens with genuine affection. "She's never once complained, even when she had every right to."

"She seemed worried about her job if you were forced to sell," Maggie notes.

"Yes, well..." Mr. Jacoby looks down at his hands, then back up at us with unexpected vulnerability in his eyes. "The truth is, Freya doesn't know it, but I have no intention of ever selling the château. And for good reason. I've already changed the instructions of my trust to leave it to Freya when I retire."

I blink in surprise. "The entire château? To Freya?"

He nods, a small smile playing at his lips. "I have no children of my own, you see. No family to leave the property to. And Freya has poured her heart and soul into the place almost as much as I have. I can't afford to pay her the salary she truly deserves right now, but at least this way, she and Noah will have security for the future."

"That's incredibly generous," I say, genuinely touched by his kindness.

"It's what she deserves," he replies simply. "The château needs someone who understands its quirks, who loves it despite its flaws. Freya *is* that person." He leans forward, his voice dropping to a conspiratorial whisper. "But please, don't tell her. I want it to be a surprise when the time comes, and besides, I'm not planning on retiring anytime soon. At least, I wasn't until I found myself in this predicament."

Joe's ears perk up at a sound from the front of the building — voices, including one with the distinctive gravel tones of Detective Freinz. Maggie hears it too, her fingers flying across her tablet as she quickly saves her notes.

"Mr. Jacoby," I say urgently, "we believe you're being framed, and we're going to prove it. Is there anything else you can tell us that might help? Anything about Pink Patricia, Harris Hastings, or anyone else who might be involved?"

He thinks for a moment, then shakes his head. "I'm afraid not. Though I did find it odd that Pink Patricia seemed so interested in the château's plumbing, of all things. She was constantly filming in areas guests rarely see— utility rooms, the basement access points."

"The plumbing again," Maggie murmurs, adding this to her notes just as the sound of Detective Freinz's voice grows louder.

"Time to go," I whisper, and Maggie nods, tucking her tablet away.

"Thank you for your time, Mr. Jacoby," I say in a normal tone, as if we're simply concluding a pleasant social call. "We'll look into these matters further."

"Thank you, Duchess," he replies, understanding our need for discretion. "Give my regards to your husband, and tell Freya not to worry. This will all be sorted out soon."

As we turn to leave, Joe pauses, looking back at Mr. Jacoby. In a gesture that surprises even me, he approaches the cell and gently pushes his nose through the bars. Mr. Jacoby reaches out to stroke the top of Joe's massive head, a genuine smile breaking through his worry.

"You're a good judge of character, aren't you, fellow?" he

says softly. "Take care of your duchess. She has quite the mystery to solve."

We make it out of the hallway just as Detective Freinz enters the jail, his scowl deepening when he sees us. I give him my most innocuous duchess smile, the one I've practiced for cutting ribbons and shaking hands with dignitaries I secretly can't stand.

"Detective," I nod pleasantly. "Lovely facilities you have here. So... *quaint*."

His eyes narrow suspiciously. "What are you doing, Duchess? I left explicit instructions—"

"Royal authority," Maggie interjects smoothly, patting her tablet. "All quite in order, I assure you. We were just leaving."

Before he can object further, we slip past him and out the heavy wooden door into the crisp mountain air. Once we're safely out of earshot, Maggie turns to me, her expression serious.

"Pink Express," she says. "Pink Patricia has to be behind that offer."

"This case just takes turn after turn," I say, shaking my head. "Noah claims he saw a man in the kitchen of the château the night Mr. Jacoby was attacked, but the kitchen staff claims no one was there. Harris Hastings says he saw Mr. Jacoby in the equipment room, but no one else can confirm his story. Pink Patricia made a secret offer to buy the château, but failed to mention that to us... Someone is lying."

"There's something we're missing," Maggie says, frustration evident in her voice. "Why would Pink Patricia want an old château with bad plumbing? And why would Harris Hastings want to frame Mr. Jacoby?"

Joe nudges my hand with his nose, as if offering his own theory. I smile down at him, feeling a renewed sense of purpose.

"I don't know yet," I say, my mind already mapping out our next steps. "But I think it's time we had a serious talk with

Pink Patricia about her aspirations. And maybe check out those plumbing areas she was so interested in filming."

As we walk away from the fairy-tale prison holding an innocent man, I can't help but feel we're getting closer to the truth. The stolen nutcracker, Harris Hastings's accident, Detective Freinz's vendetta, Pink Patricia's mysterious offer—the pieces are there. We just need to put them together before Mr. Jacoby pays the price for someone else's scheme.

And if there's one thing Joe and I are good at, it's sniffing out the truth, no matter how deeply it's buried.

CHAPTER

Thirteen

THE SNOWFALL HAS PICKED up by the time we leave the jail, fat flakes drifting down to coat Joe's golden fur like a living Christmas decoration. He shakes himself vigorously, sending a miniature blizzard in all directions as Maggie and I shield our faces.

"I need coffee," Maggie announces, clutching her tablet to her chest to protect it from the snow. "And a place to process what we just learned."

"*Café Chaleur*," I suggest, already turning in that direction. "It's only a couple blocks away, and if I remember correctly, they have the best Christmas cookies in town."

Joe perks up at the word "cookies," his tail sweeping the snow around his paws. For a 250-pound Tibetan Mastiff with the strength to take down a lion, he has remarkably simple priorities.

The café looks even more magical in the gently falling snow— its tree-through-the-center design transformed into something from a storybook with snow dusting the branches that extend over the roof. Fairy lights twinkle from every available surface, and a hand-painted sign in the window advertises "Christmas Eve Eve Specials."

"It's cozy in here," Maggie says as we push through the door into a wave of warmth, cinnamon-scented air, and the cheerful hum of conversation. The famous tree dominates the interior, its trunk rising majestically through the floor and disappearing through the ceiling, festooned with what must be hundreds of handmade ornaments. "Do you think this place was built around the tree, or did they cut a hole in an existing building?"

"Either way, it's an insurance nightmare," I reply, imagining Jack's expression if I suggested cutting a hole in Castle Atwood's roof for aesthetic purposes. The thought makes me smile despite the seriousness of our investigation.

We find a small table near the back, and Joe settles himself underneath, somehow managing to fold his enormous frame into a space that should logically be too small for him. A server approaches almost immediately, barely batting an eye at my giant dog— apparently, the Duchess of Atwood and her oversized companion are no longer news in Floconville.

"What can I get you ladies?" she asks, her smile warming further when Joe gives her his best please-feed-me eyes.

"Two chestnut lattes," Maggie orders, "and do you have anything dog-friendly? Something special?"

The server's eyes light up. "We have snowman cookies that are dog-safe. No chocolate, no xylitol, just good stuff. We can serve it on a proper plate too, if he's a gentleman."

"He's royalty," I say with perfect seriousness. "He expects the good silver."

Joe, understanding he's being discussed, thumps his tail against the floor with such enthusiasm that the neighboring table's coffee cups rattle.

Once our server leaves, Maggie pulls out her tablet and gets straight to business. "Pink Express," she says, her fingers flying across the screen. "Let's see what we can find."

I watch as she navigates through business registry

websites and financial databases that I'm fairly certain the general public isn't supposed to access.

"Got it," she announces after a few minutes, just as our server returns with two steaming mugs of chestnut latte and a snowman cookie on an actual silver dish for Joe, who accepts this offering with what can only be described as regal dignity. "Pink Express is a shell company owned by... surprise, surprise... Patricia Pinkerton, known professionally as Pink Patricia."

"So she *did* make an offer on the château," I say, wrapping my hands around the warm mug. The latte is perfect— rich and sweet, with just enough nuttiness to balance the sweetness. "But why? And why hide behind a shell company?"

Maggie takes a sip of her latte, leaving a small foam mustache that she quickly wipes away. "Let's see what Ms. Pink is up to these days." She taps a few more times, then turns her tablet to face me. "Look familiar?"

On the screen, Pink Patricia beams at the camera, her pink-clad figure standing in front of what appears to be an ancient Italian villa. The video title reads "Pink Patricia's Passport: Tuscan Villa Transformation!"

"Play it," I say, leaning closer.

Maggie taps the screen, and Pink Patricia's voice fills our corner of the café, though thankfully Maggie keeps the volume low enough that we don't disturb the other patrons.

"Ciao, my lovelies!" on-screen Patricia trills, spinning in a circle with her arms outstretched. "Welcome to the latest episode of Pink Patricia's Passport! Today, we're exploring this absolutely gorgeously dilapidated fifteenth-century villa that needs some serious Pink love!"

We watch as she prances through the villa, pointing out architectural features with surprising knowledge, then transitions to showing "before and after" segments where crumbling walls become gleaming showpieces and ancient plumbing is replaced with modern fixtures.

"Wait," I say, reaching out to tap the screen. "Go back. There was something..."

Maggie rewinds the video, and I point when I see what caught my attention. "There. She's talking to someone off-camera."

We listen closely as Patricia gestures enthusiastically at a wall. "Just like we discussed, honey bear! We'll knock through here, expose those original beams, and create a feature wall that honors the heritage while bringing in modern touches. The viewers are going to eat this up!"

"Honey bear," Maggie repeats, raising an eyebrow. "Isn't that what she calls Harris?"

"Keep watching," I urge.

Sure enough, a few moments later, the camera pans to reveal Harris Hastings in tight jeans and a tool belt, looking distinctly uncomfortable but gamely swinging a sledge-hammer at the designated wall.

"Perfect!" she squeals, clapping her hands. "This is why it's great dating an athlete! Those muscles aren't just for show, folks!"

Maggie pauses the video, her expression thoughtful. "So they've done this before. They've rehabbed old buildings on her channel."

"And this series is getting more views than any of her others," I say, pointing at the screen. "Which explains her interest in the château's plumbing. She's not just a travel vlogger— she's getting the most views from the renovation series. And the château would be her biggest project yet."

"But why would she need to sabotage Harris, her own boyfriend?" Maggie asks, scrolling through more videos showing the couple transforming various properties. "And why steal the nutcracker? None of this makes sense."

I take another sip of my latte, the pieces turning over in my mind. "Remember what Harris said during that interview at the Games? About how this competition was particularly important to him personally, and if it was his last, he wanted to make it epic for the fans?"

"You think he's planning to retire and go into property development full-time with her?" Maggie suggests.

"Maybe." I watch Joe finish his cookie with surgical precision, saving the snowman's carrot nose for last. "But that still doesn't explain why Patricia would hurt her own business partner and boyfriend."

"Unless..." Maggie taps her tablet thoughtfully. "Unless they're not actually together anymore. What if the relationship is just for show now? Maybe they've split personally but are keeping up appearances for their brand."

It's a plausible theory, but something about it doesn't sit right with me. "The way she screamed when he fell—that wasn't fake, Maggie. That was real fear."

"Then maybe she didn't know about the sabotage," Maggie counters. "Maybe someone else is involved. Detective Freinz and his brother, perhaps?"

I nod slowly, but my instincts are pulling me in another direction. "There's still the nutcracker. Why steal it? It's valuable, sure, but 50,000 euros is pocket change compared to what the château is worth."

"Insurance fraud, like Detective Freinz suggested?" Maggie offers without much conviction.

"Maybe." I stare at the remaining foam in my latte cup. "Or maybe it's a distraction. Something to keep everyone looking in the wrong direction."

Maggie finishes her latte and glances at her watch. "We should head back. Jack and the others will be wondering where we are."

I nod, but as we gather our things and Joe unfolds himself from beneath the table, I notice a small shop attached to the café—a gift boutique filled with local crafts and Christmas ornaments.

"You go ahead," I tell Maggie. "There's something I want to check out."

She gives me a knowing look. "Christmas shopping for Jack? In the middle of an investigation?"

"A girl can multitask," I reply with a small smile. "I'll meet you back at the château."

As Maggie leaves, Joe and I head for the gift shop, where something in the window display has caught my eye—something that reminds me of a conversation about dreams and futures and countryside retreats. After all, even a duchess detective on her honeymoon should take a moment for romance now and then.

———

The château rises from the darkening landscape like a fairy tale illustration, its windows glowing amber against the twilight as Joe and I make our way up the winding path. Snow crunches beneath my boots, and my breath forms little clouds that disappear into the deepening blue of evening. I'm tired after our day of investigation, but my steps quicken when I think of Jack waiting inside.

Joe trots ahead of me, his massive body somehow managing to look both dignified and eager as we approach the entrance. His internal clock has an unerring accuracy when it comes to dinner time, honeymoon or not.

The main hall is quiet when we enter, the usual bustle of guests and staff subdued this evening. Perhaps everyone is out enjoying the pre-Christmas Eve festivities in the village, or maybe they're simply giving the "crime château" a wide berth after Mr. Jacoby's arrest. Either way, the stillness feels eerie after the warmth of the café.

"Jack?" I call out, unwinding my scarf as Joe shakes off the last of the snow from his golden coat.

No answer comes, but Joe's ears perk up and he pads

purposefully toward the library. I follow, wondering if Jack has fallen asleep waiting for me. It wouldn't be the first time a royal engagement had left him exhausted enough to doze off in an armchair with a book on his chest.

The library door is slightly ajar, a warm light spilling through the crack. As I push it open, the scent hits me first — rosemary, garlic, and something rich and savory that makes my stomach immediately remind me I've had nothing but latte and a stolen bite of Joe's cookie since breakfast.

"There you are," Jack says, rising from where he's been arranging something on a small table set before the fireplace. "I was beginning to worry you'd been kidnapped by nutcracker thieves."

The library has been transformed. The heavy curtains are drawn against the night, creating an intimate cocoon of warmth and light. A fire crackles in the hearth, its flames dancing over the spines of ancient books lining the walls. The table Jack has set is draped in cream linen and set with what appears to be the château's finest china, complete with crystal wine glasses that catch the firelight. Luma lies curled up on a plush rug near the fire, her elegant form the perfect comple-ment to the refined setting.

"What's all this?" I ask, unable to keep the surprise from my voice as Joe ambles over to greet Luma with a gentle nudge of his massive head.

Jack's smile is part boyish pride, part genuine pleasure at my reaction. "I thought my detective duchess deserved a proper honeymoon dinner, even if she's busy solving international incidents." He gestures to the spread on the table. "All your favorites, prepared by yours truly."

"*You* cooked?" I step closer, taking in the dishes with growing amazement. There's a steaming bowl of French onion soup—my absolute weakness—alongside a perfectly roasted chicken with herbs, crusty bread, and what appears to be my mother's recipe for scalloped potatoes. "When did you learn to make all this?"

"I may have gotten some guidance from the kitchen staff," Jack admits, pulling out my chair with a flourish. "But I did the actual cooking. Burned myself twice for authenticity." He holds up his hand, showing a small red mark on his thumb that makes me laugh and shake my head. "I'm practicing for when we get to like as a normal couple, without all the attendants and help at our beck and call."

"I can't wait to be normal with you," I say, taking a seat me before the feast.

"You say that now, but perhaps wait until you've tried the burned bread I baked," he counters, taking his own seat and reaching for the wine. As he pours a glass, he asks me for the latest. "Alright, fill me in on the case— have you solved it?"

I tell Jack about the case while we work our way through the soup, which is actually delicious—rich and savory with the perfect amount of cheese melted on top. Jack listens intently, occasionally asking questions or making observations that remind me why I love him. He's not just humoring me; he's genuinely engaged in the investigation, his mind as sharp as mine when it comes to connecting dots.

"So Pink Patricia made an offer on the château through her shell company," he summarizes, serving me a portion of the roasted chicken that smells divine. "And she has a home renovation show with Harris as her muscle-bound co-host."

"Exactly," I say, taking a bite of chicken that confirms my husband has hidden talents. "But that still doesn't explain why Harris would identify Mr. Jacoby as the person who sabotaged his skis, or why anyone would steal the nutcracker."

Jack's eyes light up the way they do when he's about to reveal something important. "Funny you should mention that. Benjamin and I weren't just cooking all day— we did some investigating of our own." He winks at me, and it makes my heart stop.

"Is that so?" I raise an eyebrow, reaching for my wine glass. "And what did the Duke Detective and his loyal side-kick Benjamin discover?"

"We went down to the village sports pub," Jack says, looking rather pleased with himself. "Benjamin's quite good at getting people to talk, especially after I bought a round for the house. Did you know he does a remarkably accurate impression of Indiana Jones ordering a beer?"

I laugh, picturing it. "I'm not surprised. So what did you learn between impressions and free drinks?"

Jack leans forward, lowering his voice as if we might be overheard despite being alone. "Freya's ex-husband doesn't just run a gambling operation—he specializes in sports betting, particularly winter sports. And apparently, Harris Hastings was one of his regular customers."

I set down my fork, my mind immediately racing to connect this new piece of information. "Harris was betting on his own competitions?"

"Worse," Jack says grimly. "According to the locals, he was betting against himself. Losing or winning intentionally to win big."

"That would destroy his career if it got out," I murmur, the implications sinking in. "But what does that have to do with Mr. Jacoby or the château?"

Jack shrugs, spearing a potato. "That's where the trail went cold. But it's a connection we didn't have before, isn't it?"

The pieces turn in my head like a puzzle box looking for the right alignment. Harris's financial problems, his cryptic comments about this possibly being his last competition, Pink Patricia's interest in the château, Freya's ex-husband's gambling operation... Then, it hits me.

I know who stole the nutcracker.

"You're incredible," I say, leaning across the table and kissing Jack. "I think you may have just solved my case.

"I am?" Jack says, laughing. "Do I know… who did it?"

"No, but I think I do," I say, reaching across the table to squeeze Jack's hand gratefully. "I only need to confirm a couple of details, but if they reveal what I think they will, then this case is closed, which means we can get back to our honeymoon. And I need to talk to Officer Basilier tomorrow. Before the awards ceremony at the Glacial Games."

"Of course," Jack nods, turning his hand to hold mine properly. "Just promise me you'll be careful. Harris might not take kindly to you digging into his gambling habits."

"I'm always careful," I protest, which earns me a raised eyebrow from Jack and what I swear is a snort of disbelief from Joe, who has settled beside Luma near the fire.

"Speaking of tomorrow," Jack says, refilling our wine glasses, "it's Christmas Eve. Our first as husband and wife."

The reminder sends a warm flutter through me that has nothing to do with the excellent wine. "I didn't forget," I say. "This investigation has taken over everything."

"Not everything," Jack says softly. His eyes meet mine across the table, and I'm struck again by how lucky I am to have found this man who understands me so completely.

"I got you something," I say, suddenly remembering the small package in my coat pocket. I retrieve it, returning to the table with the carefully wrapped gift. "It's not much, but when I saw it, I thought of our conversation."

Jack unwraps it carefully, his face softening as he reveals the ornament— a hand-painted ceramic farmhouse nestled among rolling hills, with tiny sheep dotting the landscape. It's a perfect miniature of the retirement dream he described to me, right down to the smoke curling from the chimney.

"Rebecca," he says, his voice thick with emotion as he turns the ornament in his hands. "It's perfect."

"I thought maybe we could hang it on our tree at Castle

Atwood when we get back," I suggest. "As a reminder of what we're working toward. A normal life."

He nods, still examining the tiny details of the farmhouse. "Life changes so quickly," he says after a moment. "One day you're a bachelor duke wondering if you'll ever find someone who sees past the title, the next you're married to an animal trainer turned detective who buys you farmhouse ornaments while investigating thefts and sabotage."

I laugh, though his words touch something deeper in me. "Is that a complaint, Your Grace?"

"The opposite." He sets the ornament down carefully and takes my hand again. "It's gratitude. For you, for this life we're building—adventures and all." The moment stretches between us, warm and perfect. Jack smiles, raising his glass in a toast. "To my brilliant detective duchess," he says. "May she always find the missing pieces—and remember to take her husband along for backup."

I clink my glass against his, feeling a renewed sense of purpose along with a deep appreciation for this man who supports my every adventure.

CHAPTER
Fourteen

THE NEXT MORNING, light filters through the château library's tall windows. I stand in the doorway, taking in the scene where it all began – the stolen nutcracker, Mr. Jacoby's attack, the first domino that set this whole investigation in motion. Joe presses against my leg, his amber eyes scanning the room with the same intensity I feel. Unlike last night, when Jack transformed this space into our romantic honeymoon dinner, today the library feels like what it truly is: a crime scene waiting to reveal its secrets.

"You're staring at the room like it personally offended you," Maggie says, appearing beside me with her tablet already powered up. Her braids are pulled back in a neat bun today, and she's dressed in what I've come to recognize as her serious investigation outfit– dark pants, sensible boots, and a sweater that somehow manages to be both professional and festive with its subtle silver threading.

"Just gathering my thoughts," I reply, stepping into the library with Joe at my side. "I need to solve this case so I can get back to having an *actual* honeymoon."

Maggie smiles knowingly. "Jack mentioned your romantic dinner. Very smooth of him."

"He has his moments," I admit, feeling a small flutter in my chest at the memory of last night. The tiny farmhouse ornament is now safely tucked in my suitcase, wrapped in tissue paper, a tangible promise of our someday future. But for now, there's a case to solve and an innocent man sitting in a fairy tale jail cell.

I scan the library, taking in the details I missed during our dinner. The high vaulted ceiling with exposed wooden beams. The wall-to-wall bookshelves filled with leather-bound volumes that probably cost more than my entire education. The antique desk where Mr. Jacoby was found, now meticulously cleaned of blood but still positioned exactly as it was that day, according to the crime scene photos Maggie pulled from Detective Freinz's files. (Don't ask how she got them – some questions are better left unasked when it comes to Maggie's technical wizardry.)

"Where's Officer Basilier?" I ask, noticing our normally punctual police escort is missing.

Maggie glances at her watch. "She said she'd be here. Though she did mention something about a spa appointment she was trying to reschedule."

I shake my head in disbelief. "Vacation mode Basilier is still throwing me off. I'm half expecting her to show up with a mimosa and a massage therapist."

"She does seem to be embracing the lifestyle," Maggie agrees, setting up her tablet on a side table to take notes. "But I texted her that you specifically requested her presence. That seemed to get her attention."

As if summoned by our conversation, Officer Basilier appears in the doorway. The transformation is still jarring – her tactical black replaced by a fashionable winter outfit in shades of burgundy, her hair styled in soft waves, and those perfectly manicured nails still sporting tiny festive snowflakes. But there's something different today – a sharpness in her eyes that reminds me of the Officer Basilier I know.

"You called, I came," she announces, scanning the library with professional assessment despite her vacation attire. "Though I want it noted that I canceled an arctic berry facial for this. It was booked three months in advance."

"Your sacrifice is appreciated," I say with complete sincerity. "We need you, Officer."

"Perhaps you don't," she says, shrugging and looking at the floor. "You've solved cases without me before. Maybe what Freinz said is true and it's time to hang up my hat."

Suddenly, it hits me. *Officer Basilier has been having an existential crisis, and I've been too busy solving a crime and having a honeymoon to notice.* I step forward and put my hand on her shoulder.

"You are the best teammate an investigator could ask for, and the pride of the Monrovian police force," I say, shaking my head. "You have saved us more times than I can count, from bullets, crazed kidnappers, and by using your taser with reckless abandon." I look her dead in the eye. "Don't retire. We need you."

"*Monrovia* needs you!" Maggie adds.

Officer Basilier blinks, trying to keep a certain wetness in her eyes from spreading down her cheeks. She coughs a little, trying to hide what I think is an emotional sob. "Well," she says, straightening her shoulders. "No reason to get all emotional about it, Orange. If you really want my help all you had to do was say so." Then, she steps further into the room with a determined look I recognize. "Fill me in. What's the latest?"

"We're looking for connections," I say, moving toward the area where Mr. Jacoby was found. "Something we've missed. The nutcracker was stolen from this room, and Mr. Jacoby was attacked here. Noah says there was a man in the kitchen earlier, but no one else saw him. Harris claims Mr. Jacoby was in the equipment room at the games, but no one can corroborate his story. Pink Patricia is trying to buy the castle, and Detective Freinz has been after it for years."

"And you think the answer is still here?" Officer Basilier asks, skepticism coloring her tone.

"I think we haven't been asking the right questions," I reply, circling the desk slowly. Joe follows me, his nose occasionally dropping to the floor as if he too is searching for clues. "The water, for instance."

Maggie looks up from her tablet. "Water?"

"When Mr. Jacoby was found, there was water on the floor," I explain, recalling the initial report. "We barely paid attention to it because we were all so focused on the blood. We all thought he'd been attacked. But what if he hadn't been attacked at all?"

I kneel down, running my hand along the polished hardwood floor. It's immaculate now, but I can still see the crime scene photos in my mind – Mr. Jacoby sprawled beside the desk, a small puddle of water nearby.

"The château has plumbing issues," I continue, standing back up. "Mr. Jacoby mentioned it, Detective Freinz cited it in his building violations, and Pink Patricia was suspiciously interested in it."

Officer Basilier's eyes light up with understanding. "You think there was a leak?"

"I think it's worth checking," I say, looking up at the ceiling. The wooden beams crisscross overhead, dark with age and gleaming with what should be nothing more than generations of polish. But there, just above where the desk sits, I notice a slightly darker patch that doesn't match the rest.

"Maggie, is there a ladder around?" I ask, my eyes still fixed on the ceiling.

"I'll check," she says, disappearing into the hallway.

Officer Basilier follows my gaze. "You see something?"

"Maybe," I murmur, moving to stand directly beneath the

darker spot. "The ceiling here is original to the building, right? Hundreds of years old?"

"According to the château brochure," she confirms. "Part of its historic charm and why it's protected by the historical society."

Maggie returns, followed by a staff member carrying a wooden library ladder – the rolling kind that belongs on a movie set about eccentric book collectors. "Will this work?" she asks.

"Perfect," I say, waiting for the staff member to position it beneath the spot I've been studying. Joe watches with interest as I kick off my boots – climbing a ladder in snow-dampened footwear seems like a recipe for disaster – and begin my ascent.

The ladder creaks slightly under my weight but holds firm. As I near the top, the detail of the ceiling comes into sharper focus, and what I suspected becomes undeniable.

"There's mold," I announce, carefully reaching out to touch the discolored patch. The wood feels damp beneath my fingers, the dark stain spreading in a pattern that suggests water damage. "Recent too, from the looks of it."

"Mold?" Maggie repeats, typing rapidly. "Above where Mr. Jacoby was found?"

"Exactly." I examine the surrounding area more closely, noting how the mold follows a straight line across one of the beams. "There's a pipe running through here, isn't there? Behind the ceiling?"

Officer Basilier nods, professional interest fully engaged now. "Most of these old buildings have the plumbing retrofitted above the ceilings or behind the walls. Preserves the historic integrity while allowing for modern convenience."

I carefully make my way back down the ladder, my mind racing. "So there was a leak. The day the nutcracker was stolen and Mr. Jacoby was attacked, water was dripping from the ceiling – or at least seeping through enough to create that puddle."

"But what does that have to do with the theft?" Maggie asks, frowning at her notes.

"Nothing," I admit, slipping my boots back on. And that might be the point." I turn to Maggie. "I need to know where Freya and Noah are right now."

Maggie checks her tablet. "According to the staff schedule, they're at the Glacial Games finals. Freya mentioned yesterday they never miss the closing ceremonies, and Mr. Jacoby gave them VIP passes this year."

"Harris Hastings would have access to a private box at the Games, wouldn't he?" I ask, remembering how celebrities and athletes often watch from exclusive areas when not competing.

"Definitely," Officer Basilier confirms. "All the top athletes get private viewing areas for their teams and sponsors."

"Then that's where we need to go," I say with sudden certainty. "Right now, to Harris Hastings's private box at the Glacial Games finals."

Maggie looks surprised. "Now?"

"Now" I confirm, already heading for the door with Joe at my heels. "Call Jack, Benjamin, and anyone else who can meet us there."

"On it," she says, fingers flying across her tablet as we move.

Officer Basilier falls into step beside me, all traces of her vacation persona now completely submerged beneath her professional demeanor. "You know who did it."

"I think I do," I confirm, putting a hand on her shoulder. "And if we can corner all our suspects in a VIP box at the game, I can share my theory and see how their behavior confirms it. Which means I'll need you there, ready to arrest them." I smile at her. "That is, *if* you can postpone the spa appointment…"

Officer Basilier salutes me. "Officer Basilier, reporting for duty." Then, she offers me something rare: a smile. "Thanks for seeing me, Orange."

As we step outside into the crisp mountain air, I feel the familiar rush of an investigation nearing its conclusion. Joe bounds ahead, seemingly as eager as I am to get to the Games and confront our suspects.

"Maggie," I call over my shoulder as we hurry toward the waiting car, "tell Jack to meet us at Harris's box. And make sure he brings Luma – we might need all the canine backup we can get."

CHAPTER

Fifteen

HARRIS HASTINGS'S private box at the Glacial Games screams "I'm important" with its plush seating, panoramic views, and champagne on ice that nobody's touched. A view of the ski slopes extends above the box's edge, all mountains and pine trees. Joe stays close to my side as we enter, his massive body creating a natural pathway through the startled group already assembled inside. Everyone is here, as requested. Tension clings to the air.

Exactly the vibe I was hoping for.

I catch Jack's gaze across the room, where he stands with Luma beside him, both of them looking equally alert and concerned. Game time.

Harris himself reclines in what looks like a custom-designed chair, his injured leg elevated on a cushioned ottoman, the cast gleaming white against the dark upholstery. Pink Patricia hovers nearby in a shade of pink so bright it practically vibrates, her phone for once nowhere in sight. Freya stands awkwardly near the window, her hand resting protectively on Noah's shoulder. The boy looks like he might be sick, his complexion the color of old snow, eyes darting nervously around the room.

"What is the meaning of this?" Pink Patricia demands, her usually perky voice sharp with annoyance. "Harris needs rest, not an audience. The doctor specifically said—"

"It's fine," Harris interrupts, his gaze fixed on me with unexpected intensity. "Let's see what the *Duchess* has to say." He emphasizes the word "duchess" as if he's reminding me of an important fact about myself.

Benjamin steps forward from where he's been standing beside Jack, his excitement barely contained. "This is like the end of a mystery movie," he stage-whispers to nobody in particular. "When the detective gathers all the suspects!"

"We're not suspects," Pink Patricia snaps, though there's a flicker of something uncertain in her eyes. "Uhm, are we?" When nobody answers, she rattles on. "We're victims here! Someone deliberately sabotaged Harris's skis!"

Before I can respond, the door to the box swings open again and Detective Freinz strides in, his perpetual scowl deepening when he spots our gathering. "What is this circus?" he demands, his gravelly voice cutting through the room. "I received a message that there was new evidence regarding the Jacoby case. I didn't expect an ambush—"

He stops mid-sentence, his eyes widening as the door opens once more and Officer Basilier enters, followed by none other than Mr. Jacoby himself, looking rumpled but remarkably composed for a man who was in jail just hours ago.

"What the hell?" Detective Freinz explodes, his face flushing dark red. "Jacoby is supposed to be in police custody. Who authorized his release?"

Officer Basilier steps forward, all traces of her vacation persona completely gone. She's back in her tactical uniform, though I notice she's kept the festive nails. "I did," she says coolly. "After presenting evidence— compliments of the Duchess— to Judge Moreau that contradicts your entire case. The judge is a personal friend I've made through years of service. Years I don't plan on throwing away just because of one little man."

"*Evidence*?" Detective Freinz sneers. "What evidence could possibly—"

"Perhaps," I interject, moving to the center of the room with Joe at my side, "we should start at the beginning. If everyone would please take a seat?"

There's a moment of hesitation, then a shuffling as people find chairs, with Detective Freinz remaining stubbornly on his feet. Mr. Jacoby takes a seat near Freya, who looks at him with such relief it's almost painful to witness. Noah, however, won't meet anyone's eyes, his gaze fixed firmly on his shoes.

"Thank you all for coming," I begin, feeling Jack's reassuring presence behind me. "Over the past few days, we've been investigating the theft of a valuable nutcracker from Château des Flocons and the subsequent attack on Mr. Jacoby. What seemed like a simple theft has revealed itself to be something much more complex— a web of motives, opportunities, and secrets that involves almost everyone in this room."

I turn to Detective Freinz, who's watching me with barely concealed contempt. "Detective, you were convinced from the start that Mr. Jacoby orchestrated these events himself, possibly as insurance fraud. But your conviction wasn't based on evidence— it was based on your brother's desire to acquire the château for his real estate portfolio."

Freinz's face contorts. "That's absurd. I was following the evidence—"

"You were following your ambition," Officer Basilier cuts in. "We have records of your brother's multiple lowball offers for the property, all rejected by Mr. Jacoby. We also have witnesses who heard you threatening Mr. Jacoby at the Glacial Games."

Freinz opens his mouth to protest, but I continue before he

can speak. "But you weren't the only one interested in getting control of the château. Was he, Pink Patricia?"

All eyes turn to her, and she blinks rapidly, one hand flying to her throat. "I don't know what you mean."

"Pink Express," I say simply. "Your shell company made an offer on the château just last week. Well above market value, but still anonymous. Why the secrecy?"

Harris shifts in his chair, wincing slightly. "It was supposed to be a surprise," he says, his voice weary. "For my retirement."

"That's right," I nod. "Harris Hastings, four-time champion, was planning to retire after these Games. But not because he wanted to— because he *had* to. Your endorsements have been drying up, haven't they? After that poor performance last season, your sponsors started dropping you one by one. But we have to ask… *why* the poor performance? You're a talented skier, after all…" I pause for effect, letting the question dangle. "Harris, you were throwing competitions on purpose every now and then to get an extra pay day, weren't you?

Harris's jaw tightens, but he doesn't deny it.

"You worked with a gambling ring outside of town, coincidentally run by none other than Noah's father."

Freya gasps, covering her mouth with her hand. Noah looks at the ground as if he wishes he were anywhere else.

"The Glacial Games was your final, big con," I turn back to Harris. "You planned to throw the games, as you have many other events, and collect a bribe from the gambling, along with your own debts. You tampered with your own boot, and tried to make it look like an accident."

"But why lie about my presence?" Mr. Jacoby says to Harris, affronted. "If you wanted to cheat, that's one thing, but why blame *me?*"

Harris looks away.

"Because he knew Detective Freinz had it out for you," I

say to Mr. Jacoby. "The gambling ring Harris was involved in is run by Noah's father, who undoubtedly told him all about the Château and his ex-wife's unstable employment there."

"He knows everything," Freya nods, looking angry at herself. "I shouldn't have told him so much, Mr. Jacoby. I never thought it would lead to something like this! I was explaining to him that he has to support his child—"

"Freya, this is not your fault, my dear," Mr. Jacoby says warmly.

"Harris found out about the Château and told his girl-friend, Pink Patricia," I continue. "And together, they saw an opportunity. Isn't that right? The two of you would buy Château des Flocons, renovate it like you've done with other historic properties, and turn it into the backdrop for your next career phase. 'Pink Patricia's Château Makeover,' featuring retired skiing legend Harris Hastings as your muscle-bound co-host.'"

Pink Patricia moves closer to Harris, resting a protective hand on his shoulder.

"Is that a crime?" Pink Patricia challenges, her voice rising. "Having a business plan?"

"No," I admit. "But what happened next crosses several legal lines. You were the only skiers in the games who decided to stay at the Château, and it wasn't because you appreciate quaint architecture. You weren't just here as guests, were you? You were conducting a covert inspection of the property. That's why you were so interested in the plumbing, Patricia. You were documenting the issues, calculating reno-vation costs, planning how to turn this 'money pit,' as Mr. Jacoby called it, into your next profitable project for your series."

Maggie steps forward, her tablet ready. "We have first-hand accounts of you filming in restricted areas of the château — the kitchen, utility closets, basement access points…"

Pink Patricia's cheeks flush to match her outfit. "I was just creating content for my followers," she insists, though her voice lacks conviction.

Harris says nothing, but his face has gone pale beneath his perfect tan. Pink Patricia looks between him and me, confusion and betrayal warring on her face.

"...and Detective Freinz," I continue, "... had such a vendetta against Mr. Jacoby, he failed to perform a thorough investigation of the crime. And *also* failed to notice his competition right in front of him, scoping out the very château he'd been hunting for years."

Detective Freinz looks as if I've hit him over the head with a frying pan. His mustache seems to curl in on itself, and he leans against the wall for support.

"But none of that explains who stole the nutcracker or attacked Mr. Jacoby," Benjamin points out, clearly trying to move the story along.

"You're right," I agree, my heart heavy with what comes next. "Despite all these schemes and plans, neither Harris, Pink Patricia, *nor* Detective Freinz were responsible for what happened in the library that night." I turn slowly, my gaze landing on Noah, who seems to shrink under the weight of it. "Were they, Noah?"

Freya gasps, her hand flying to her mouth. "What? No, that's impossible. Noah was in his room studying—"

"No, Mom," Noah says, his voice barely above a whisper. "I wasn't."

The silence that follows is absolute, broken only by Joe's soft whine as he senses the boy's distress.

"Tell them what happened," I say gently. "It's time for the truth."

Noah's eyes fill with tears, his shoulders slumping in defeat. "I stole the nutcracker," he admits, his voice breaking. "But I didn't hurt Mr. Jacoby! I swear I didn't! It was an accident!"

Freya looks stricken, her face ashen. "Noah, why? Why would you do such a thing?"

"Because of Dad," Noah says, tears now streaming freely down his face. "He stopped sending money for school. He said he couldn't afford it anymore, but I saw on social media that he bought a new car! And I heard you on the phone with the school administration, Mom. I heard you say we might have to move because you couldn't afford the tuition on your own."

He wipes furiously at his tears with the sleeve of his too-small snowboard jacket. "I knew the nutcracker was valuable. I heard Mr. Jacoby telling a guest it would sell for 50,000 euros at auction. I thought... I thought if I could sell it, we could stay here. I could stay at my school. We wouldn't have to leave."

"Oh, Noah," Freya whispers, her own eyes welling up. "You didn't!"

"I was careful," Noah continues, the words pouring out of him now. "I waited until everyone was busy. I know all the staff routines. I used to help Mr. Jacoby with security checks when I was younger." He looks at Mr. Jacoby with such remorse it's heartbreaking. "I'm so sorry, Mr. Jacoby. I didn't mean for anyone to get hurt. Especially not you."

"And you lied about seeing someone in the kitchen, didn't you?" I prompt gently. "Because our questions made you nervous."

Noah nods. "I made up a man because I thought maybe it would take the attention away from me. I just wished it were true. That I could undo what I'd done and make it so somebody else did it."

"Noah, what really happened that day?" I press.

Noah sniffs, composing himself slightly. "I went to the library. I knew where the nutcracker was kept. I had it in my hands when I heard someone coming. I panicked and hid behind the curtains."

"It was me you heard," Mr. Jacoby says quietly. "Coming to polish the case."

Noah nods miserably. "You came in and turned on the light. I was going to stay hidden until Mr. Jacoby left, but then he walked toward the desk where the nutcracker display case had been. He was going to see it was missing. I thought maybe I could sneak out while his back was turned, but then..."

"But then he slipped on water that was on the library floor," I finish for him, the final piece clicking into place. "On water from the leaking pipe overhead."

Mr. Jacoby looks stunned. "I didn't remember how I fell," he says, shocked at his own hidden history. "I just assumed I was attacked, but—" he glances at Detective Freinz. "I guess Freinz was right about the plumbing," Mr. Jacoby says, horrified. "It really *is* dangerous."

"Is that what happened, Noah?" I ask.

"Yes," Noah whispers. "I saw Mr. Jacoby slip on water from the leak. He fell so hard. There was blood. I didn't know what to do. I was so scared. I wanted to help him but I wasn't sure how. I put the nutcracker in my backpack and ran, looking for my Mom to tell her, but I couldn't find her."

"Because I was giving the group tour to all of you," Freya fills in. "And we discovered Mr. Jacoby only moments later."

"Noah," I say gently. "Where is the nutcracker?"

Noah deflates miserably. Then, he reaches over his shoulder and pulls his backpack off his back, dropping it on the floor. He reaches inside and pulls out an ancient looking nutcracker, dotted in signatures. The painted surface is chipped and waxy, the nutcracker's wooden limbs loose at their joints. The autographs scrawl across the lacquer in different inks, crowding over old cracks and stains, the ink looking too "new" against old acrylic paint.

"I've been— carrying it around—" Noah says, crying in between the words. "I just keep trying to find—" he hiccups.

"The right moment— to tell— but—" He fully breaks down, running to his Mom and burying himself in her arms.

His thin shoulders shake. Freya wraps her arms around him, her own tears falling silently. "Mr. Jacoby," she says, "I'm so sorry. I had no idea. We'll make this up to you. We'll—"

Mr. Jacoby holds a hand in the air, silencing her. Then he rises from his chair, moving slowly to stand before Noah. The boy can't meet his eyes, staring instead at the floor between them.

"Noah," Mr. Jacoby says, his voice gentle but firm. "Look at me."

Reluctantly, Noah raises his head.

"Life changes are hard," Mr. Jacoby continues. "They're scary and unpredictable, and sometimes they make us do things we wouldn't normally do."

"Don't I know it," Officer Basilier mutters, examining her festive nails with sudden interest. "I almost retired because of one comment from a fat man with a mustache."

Detective Freinz looks at her, piecing together that he is, in fact, that fat man.

"But the spirit of Christmas," Mr. Jacoby continues, "is about being together and supporting each other through those changes." He places a hand on Noah's shoulder.

"Am I going to jail?" Noah says, shaking. "I left you on the floor. I should have called an ambulance."

"I'm afraid I landed on the floor because of my own inability to fix the plumbing. And you're not going to jail," Mr. Jacoby says, laughing. "I'm not going to press charges."

"You're not?" Noah asks, disbelief cutting through his tears.

"No," Mr. Jacoby smiles. "In fact, I think it's clear that I could use *more* help with the château, not less. Freya," he turns to her, "I've been meaning to offer you a promotion for some time now. A significant one, with an equally significant salary increase. I'd like you to take over running the daily operations of the château, effective immediately."

Freya stares at him, speechless.

"And Noah," Mr. Jacoby adds, turning back to the boy, "I think, perhaps, if your Mom is open to it, you could help around the Château on weekends for extra money. A job, perhaps?"

"Really?" Noah says.

"An excellent idea," Jack clears his throat, taking on a Duke-ly posture. "The Monrovian crown would be glad to push more funds your way," Jack interjects, giving Mr. Jacoby a familial nod. "I'm sure we could find the resources. And this means you won't have to leave your school. Or your home."

"But," Noah protests weakly, "after what I did..."

"What you did was wrong," Mr. Jacoby says firmly. "But it was also an act of love and desperation to protect your home and your future. I understand that better than most." He glances around the room, his gaze lingering briefly on Detective Freinz. "Some people see the château as just a property to be acquired. You see it as a home worth fighting for. That means something to me. This is what Christmas is about, son. Grace. Forgiving each other. And finding gifts we can give that show our care."

Noah breaks down again, this time with relief instead of fear. Freya mouths a silent "thank you" to Mr. Jacoby over her son's head.

"Well," Detective Freinz says stiffly, moving toward the door, "I suppose I should update my report." His tone suggests he's not happy about this resolution, but even he can recognize when he's been thoroughly defeated.

"I suppose you should," Officer Basilier agrees with just a touch of smugness. "I'd be happy to assist you with the proper paperwork for dismissing all charges against Mr. Jacoby."

As the detective leaves, a palpable relief sweeps through the room. Harris and Pink Patricia exchange a look that suggests they have a lot to discuss about their future plans. Harris stares at me.

"You have no formal evidence that I had any hand in throwing the competition," he says, his look deadly.

"I suppose not," I say, smiling at him. "But I suppose we both agree you've retired."

With that, Pink Patricia and Harris exit the box, him on a crutch, her helping him with a hand beneath his shoulder. Pink Patricia already has her phone in her hand, and I'm sure this won't be the last we've seen of them.

Finally, the box is just us: Jack, Maggie, Benjamin, and the dogs. Benjamin is practically vibrating with excitement at having witnessed what he keeps calling "the big reveal, just like in the movies! I feel like I was in a movie myself! I get why you love this!"

Maggie taps on her tablet one last time before tucking it away. "Mystery solved," she says with satisfaction.

Joe presses against my leg, his mission accomplished, his warm eyes looking up at me with what I swear is pride. I scratch behind his ears, grateful as always for his steady presence through this bizarre honeymoon adventure.

Jack appears at my side, his hand finding mine with familiar warmth. "Not exactly the relaxing ski trip you promised me," he says, his eyes crinkling at the corners.

"That's true," I say seriously, squeezing his hand. "Which is why I think we need to extend our trip and stay another week. This time, with no crime. Maggie?"

"Already booking the rooms!" Maggie shouts back at me, her tablet out.

"No crime this time?" Jack says, aghast. "You mean we can just enjoy a peaceful stay in a small town with no mysteries or Royal functions… just us and the dogs?"

"It's practice," I tell him. "For the future and our country-side retirement."

"Even in the future," Jack says, smiling at me. "I hope we'll find time for your adventures. I wouldn't have it any other way. You keep me on my toes, Rebecca Orange."

He kisses me, images of our future country-home dancing in both our minds.

And as the Christmas Eve sky deepens to twilight outside the windows, with medals being awarded on the slopes below and reconciliations happening all around us, I realize that Jack is right. This bizarre, chaotic, wonderful adventure is exactly the right honeymoon for us—proof that our life together will never be boring, and that sometimes, the greatest gift is simply having someone to solve life's mysteries by your side.

Joe woofs softly, as if in agreement, and Luma pads over to join us, completing our little family circle. Mystery solved, Christmas saved, and the promise of more on the horizon beckoning me forward— with all the right people next to me.

————

Keep reading for an excerpt from the next book in the Rebecca Orange series, "A Treacherous Train!"

A Treacherous Train

I press my forehead against the cool glass of the train's dining car window, watching snowflakes dance in the wind before vanishing into the white abyss below. The *Monrovian Royal Express* clings to the mountainside, navigating hairpin turns that make my stomach lurch despite the train's gentle sway. We're returning home to Atwood Village after the final week of our extended honeymoon in Floconville's winter wonderland. We've enjoyed a full seven days without crime-solving or royal duties, and I'm so refreshed I feel ready to face whatever royal challenges await us back home. *Almost.*

"Penny for your thoughts?" Jack slides his hand over mine, his wedding band catching the light from the crystal chandeliers that dangle precariously above our dining table.

"I'm thinking about how many pastries I can enjoy on the train ride home," I say, turning away from the window to face my husband—my *husband!*—the Duke of Atwood.

"I'm so glad you two got an extra week with absolutely no murders to solve," Maggie chimes in from across the table, raising her champagne flute. Her blonde braids are adorned with tiny snowflake pins, a souvenir from our time in the mountains. "A toast to the first drama-free royal vacation in Monrovian history!"

"I wouldn't call it drama-free," Officer Basilier says, sighing a little. She's seated beside Maggie and Benjamin, back in her police uniform, taser firmly holstered in her belt. "You all almost let me *retire* and barely said a word!"

"We knew you'd reach the right conclusion eventually," Maggie says, nudging Officer Basilier's arm with her own elbow so she's forced to raise her glass.

We all laugh and clink glasses. Even Joe and Luma, settled comfortably on plush velvet cushions beside our chairs, perk up their ears at the sound. The dining car of the *Monrovian Royal Express* is more luxurious any train I've ever been on— gilded mirrors line the walls, reflecting the warm glow from antique sconces. The tables are set with fine china bearing the royal crest, and even the napkins are folded into perfect swans.

"Your tea, Your Grace," a uniformed attendant says, placing a steaming cup beside Jack. Another server simultaneously sets down two silver bowls for Joe and Luma.

"Is that... filet mignon?" I ask, peering at what appears to be perfectly cooked steak in my dog's dish.

"But of course, Madame Duchess," the server says with a slight bow. "For the royal canines, we prepare only the finest cuts, lightly seared as requested."

Joe gives me a smug look— if dogs can look smug— before delicately beginning to eat. Luma, ever the proper royal pup, waits until he starts before daintily picking at her own meal.

"You know," I whisper to Jack, "I think the dogs are adjusting to royal life faster than I am."

Jack's laugh is interrupted by a particularly violent lurch of the train, causing the silverware to rattle alarmingly. Outside, the snow has intensified, whipping past the windows in white sheets.

"Mon Dieu!" Benjamin exclaims, gripping the edge of the table. "This weather is becoming very concerning, no? Like the beginning of one of your American horror films." He looks at me with wide eyes. "You know the one where the train gets stuck and there is a monster? Or was it a murderer?"

"I think you're mixing up about five different movies," I reply, trying not to let his words trigger my own overactive imagination. After all, I've had enough real-life mysteries to solve lately without inventing new ones.

He's not wrong, I think, trying not to look out the window. *The weather is a little scary.*

"The *Monrovian Royal Express* has never failed to complete its journey in its one hundred and twenty-three years of service," a deep voice announces from behind me. I turn to see the train's conductor, a distinguished man with a perfectly trimmed gray mustache and a uniform adorned with so many medals it's a wonder he can stand upright.

"Conductor Beaumont," Jack acknowledges with a nod. "I trust we're not in any danger?"

"Not at all, Your Grace." The conductor bows slightly. "This route through the mountains is treacherous, yes, but our engineers are the finest in Europe. I simply wanted to personally ensure your comfort and to inform you that we've added extra coal to the engines. We may be running a little behind schedule due to the weather, but we will arrive safely at Atwood Station in a matter of days."

"Thank you for the update," I say, trying to sound duchess-like even though I still feel like an imposter whenever someone addresses me by my new title.

"It is my honor, Madame Duchess." Conductor Beaumont bows again. "Please enjoy the remainder of your meal. Chef has prepared his famous chocolate soufflé for dessert— a special tribute to your honeymoon."

As the conductor departs, Maggie pulls out her tablet, her

expression shifting from relaxed vacation mode to efficient royal assistant.

"Speaking of our return," she says, swiping through screens, "I should probably brief you on what's waiting at Castle Atwood."

"Maggie," Jack groans, "we still have three hours on this train. Can't we pretend to be normal people for just a little longer?"

"Sorry, Your Grace," Maggie says, not looking sorry at all, "but Her Majesty the Queen has been filling my email inbox faster than I can empty it. There are at least seventeen new initiatives she wants you both to spearhead, three charity galas to attend next month, and—" Maggie pauses, glancing up with an expression that makes me instinctively reach for Jack's hand.

"And?" Jack prompts, his voice suddenly tense.

"*And* Her Majesty has requested to come stay at Castle Atwood. For an 'indefinite period of time,' according to her personal secretary." Maggie's fingers make air quotes around the words. "She's bringing your cousin Valencia with her."

Jack's teacup clatters against its saucer. "My *aunt* wants to visit? The Queen of Monrovia, who hasn't left the Royal Palace for a personal visit in over a decade, wants to stay at Castle Atwood? With Valencia?"

Even Officer Basilier, who has been quietly enjoying her meal at the end of our table, looks up with interest at this news.

"Did Her Majesty say why?" Jack asks, his brow furrowed.

Maggie scrolls through her tablet. "The official reason is that Princess Valencia could benefit from some mentorship. Whatever that means."

"Mentorship?" Jack repeats, looking increasingly alarmed. "From whom? About what?"

"The email doesn't specify," Maggie says, "but I've already begun preparations for their visit. The Queen's suite is being refreshed, and we're converting the east wing guest room for Princess Valencia."

I watch as Jack's face cycles through confusion, concern, and something close to dread. His aunt, the Queen of Monrovia, isn't known for her warmth or spontaneity. From everything Jack has told me, she's a brilliant strategist and ruler, but about as cuddly as a cactus.

"Jack," I say, placing my hand over his, "don't worry. We'll make sure everything at Castle Atwood is perfect for her visit."

"It's not that," he says, lowering his voice. "My aunt doesn't do anything without a purpose. If she's coming to Castle Atwood, bringing Valencia, and talking about 'mentorship,' there's a reason. A political reason."

"Maybe she just wants to see your new bride," Benjamin offers helpfully. "To welcome Rebecca into the family, no?"

Jack shakes his head. "The Queen sent a diamond tiara as her welcome. That was more than enough family warmth from her."

Oh yeah, the diamond tiara, I think, trying to remember where I stored the thing. An image of the beautiful wreath of diamonds comes to mind— it's shoved at the top of my closet, next to a dog-training fanny pack and a pair of beat-up old sneakers.

"Whatever her reason," I say, squeezing his hand, "we'll handle it together. The staff loves you, the village respects you, and Castle Atwood has never run more smoothly. What could possibly go wrong?"

As soon as the words leave my mouth, I regret them. Everyone at our table stares at me. Benjain's eyes are wide. Maggie's cheeks flush. Officer Basilier shakes her head like I'm the biggest moron in the world.

"Seriously, Rebecca," Maggie urges me in a whisper. "You've *got* to stop saying that!"

She's right, I think. Because if there's one thing I've learned since becoming the Duchess of Atwood, it's that tempting fate in Monrovia never ends well.

The train gives another violent lurch, and outside, the snow falls harder, obscuring the steep drop just inches from the tracks.

———

The storm has escalated from picturesque to ominous by the time we finish our dessert. Jack and I say our goodnights to Maggie, Benjamin, and Officer Basilier, who are heading to their own compartments in the car ahead of ours. I can't help but notice how the chandeliers in the dining car sway with each gust of wind that hits the train, and the once-charming clink of fine china now sounds like warning bells. Joe presses against my leg as we walk through the narrow corridor, his massive body somehow sensing my unease. Or maybe he's just reacting to the way the train keeps jolting as we climb higher into the mountains.

"Did you notice the conductor's face when he came back to check on us?" I ask Jack as we make our way toward the rear of the train where our suite is located.

"No, what about it?" Jack has Luma's leash in one hand and is steadying himself against the wall with the other as the train negotiates another sharp curve.

"He looked worried. Not 'I'm concerned about the comfort of our royal passengers' worried, but 'we might be in actual trouble' worried."

Jack raises an eyebrow. "Rebecca Orange— the Duchess of Atwood— are you looking for a mystery where there isn't one?"

"Maybe," I admit, stumbling slightly as the train lurches again. "But in my defense, mysteries do seem to find us with alarming regularity."

"Maggie's right," Jack laughs, raising an eyebrow. "You've got to stop saying things like that!"

The corridor of the Monrovian Royal Express is as opulent as the dining car— plush red carpet underfoot, polished mahogany paneling on the walls, and brass light fixtures that cast a warm glow over everything. Under normal circumstances, it would feel cozy. Tonight, with the wind howling outside and the snow pelting the windows like someone throwing handfuls of gravel, it feels like we're traversing the set of an Agatha Christie adaptation.

"Do you think Benjamin was right?" I ask, lowering my voice though there's no one else in the corridor. "About this being like the beginning of a horror movie?"

"... *another* thing you shouldn't say!" Jack laughs as if there's nothing to fear, but it sounds a bit forced. "Don't tell me the woman who faced down tigers is afraid of a little snow?"

"Not afraid," I correct him, "just... cautious. Twenty years of animal training teaches you to pay attention when things feel off."

We reach the end of the corridor where an ornate door bears a small placard reading "Snowflake Suite." It's the train's most luxurious accommodation, reserved for royalty and dignitaries.

"Well, I promise that what's behind this door is the opposite of horror," Jack says, producing a large old-fashioned key. "The Snowflake Suite has a private bathroom with an actual tub, a sitting area with a fireplace, and a bed that's reportedly so comfortable the Swedish ambassador once missed his stop because he couldn't bear to get up. You are safe and sound, in the finest accommodations the world can provide."

He's right, I let my shoulder relax as Jack slips a key into the suite's ornate lock. *I'm worrying about a little weather when it's nothing.* I'm going to step into our beautiful room and enjoy a bubble bath. Beside me, Joe and Luma wag their tails, ready to enter our home-away-from-home.

The door swings open with a soft creak that somehow cuts through the rumble of the train. Jack reaches inside to flip on the lights, and for a moment, I see what should be there— a beautifully appointed suite with velvet furnishings, gleaming woodwork, and a crackling fire in the grate.

Then my brain registers what is *actually* there.

A woman lies spread-eagled in the center of the room, her uniform—the same maroon and gold as the other train staff— twisted awkwardly around her body. Her nametag is hanging half-off her shirt pocket, the pin broken. Her eyes are open, staring at the ceiling, but there's no question that she's seeing nothing at all.

She's dead. And she's lying in the middle of our stateroom.

"Oh my God," I whisper, my hand flying to my mouth.

Jack is frozen in the doorway, one arm extended to hold me back. "Rebecca, don't—"

But it's too late. I've already seen everything— the unnatural angle of her neck, the blue tinge to her lips, the small trickle of dried blood from her chest, where a knife has been buried. Death isn't a stranger to me after years of working with predatory animals, but this is different. This is intentional. Human.

Joe lets out a low, rumbling growl, his hackles rising as he stares at the body. Beside him, Luma whimpers and tries to back away, straining against her leash.

"We need to get Basilier," Jack says, his voice dropping to the controlled, authoritative tone he uses in emergencies. "Don't touch anything."

"Jack," I say, my voice barely audible over the howling wind outside, "look at her face."

He follows my gaze, and I see the moment he notices what I've already seen— the look of shock and betrayal frozen on her features. The knife in her chest. This wasn't an accident.

The train gives another violent lurch, and for a horrible moment, I think the body is going to slide across the floor toward us. It doesn't, but the movement seems to break us both out of our stunned paralysis.

"We need to secure the scene," Jack says, reaching for the door to close it.

"And find Basilier," I confirm, already turning to head back up the corridor.

But before either of us can move, the lights flicker once, twice, and then plunge us into darkness. The only illumination comes from the snow-reflected moonlight through the windows, casting everything in a ghostly blue glow—including the dead woman on our honeymoon suite floor.

It's then that the worst part of it all comes to my mind:

Whoever did this… is still on the train.

And I'm going to find them.

———

To keep reading, look for "A Treacherous Train," available in paperback!

Dear Reader,

Thank you for dedicating your time to the world of Monrovia and Rebecca Orange! These books mean so much to me, and my hope is always that what I've written gives you the chance to escape to a cozy new place.

I love hearing from readers (seriously, it makes the job so fun!). Please reach out to me anytime by visiting www.valeriebrandy.com or finding me on social media, even if it's just to say "hi" or talk about flower names for coffee. Monrovia is special because of the community there, and I love forming the same cozy friendships around my books.

You can also join my author club mailing list for free giveaways and updates on new releases. Scan the QR Code below or visit my website to join!

Warmly,

— Valerie Brandy